THE BRITISH
ARMY BASE

TO DEHLI →

THE JUNGLE CAMP

Alexa

CW00953032

THE MAGIC LANTERN

OF KIMBUSTAN

BY J.H. LEWIS

Pen Press Publishers Ltd

First published in Great Britain by
Pen Press Publishers Ltd
25 Eastern PLace
Brighton
BN2 1GJ
www.penpress.co.uk

ISBN13: 978-1-905621-88-0

Printed and bound in the UK

A catalogue record of this book is available from
the British Library

Cover and illustrations by Alexa Garside
www.kimbustan.com

TO PHILIPPA, JONATHAN, SHOSHANA AND MIRIAM.

SOS Children's Villages

SOS Children is the world's largest orphan charity, providing a home and family for children who have no one else to turn to. SOS Children creates villages where SOS mothers provide the love, guidance and security these children need for a happy childhood.

Today there are 444 SOS Children's villages in 124 countries around the world, where over 60,000 children are given long-term care and support. Alongside the villages, SOS Children also works with local communities, providing education, healthcare, HIV/AIDS support and vocational training, benefiting almost a million people globally.

Thanks to its numerous facilities and widespread locations, SOS Children is also often at the forefront of emergency relief programmes in situations of crisis and natural disaster, most recently following the Asian tsunami and the earthquake in Kashmir.

The author is proud to dedicate this edition of "The Magic Lantern of Kimbustan" to SOS Children's Villages UK, in support of its work for orphaned and abandoned children worldwide.

TIM & KELLY

ACKNOWLEDGEMENTS AND THANKS

A number of people have helped this book along. My apologies to any I've missed.

Thank you to Kirsten, Natalie and Veronica for manuscript production and research; to Philippa and Lucy for help in proofreading; to Jon for advice on magic; and to Anant and Radhika for help on Hindi names. Thanks also to Markus, Dan, Jessica and Gemma-Claire for their helpful comments on the draft manuscript.

At Pen Press, special thanks to Lynn, Grace, Joanna, Alexa and Kathryn for help, advice and the hard work needed to turn this manuscript into print. Thanks also to Pat at Orchard and Philippa for marketing and PR.

At Chelsea House, a great deal of help and assistance was received from Sally Anne, Colin and John; David and Fay; and Jemma. A big "thank you" also to Max, Paul, Mark and Shoshana for video and website design.

Acknowledgements and thanks are due to The Magic Lantern Society for giving permission to quote from their website.

Finally, writing a first novel is never easy. Thank you to my family for listening to endless hours of bad storytelling over the years, and for their encouragement, patience and help in the birthing process.

Agnes & Irene

THE MAGIC LANTERN

"The magic lantern ... has a long and complicated history, and like lots of fascinating inventions, many people were involved in its development. No one can say for sure who invented the magic lantern. It is part of the marvellous world of optical projection and stands alongside the *Camera Obscura*, Shadow Shows and Magic Mirror."

George Auckland,
Magic Lantern Society

"Amulets – protective devices worn around the body, or placed next to other objects, to protect them from various evils."

"Traditions of Magic in Late Antiquity"
University of Michigan Library

ASHWINA & PARI

PROLOGUE

KIMBUSTAN, INDIA.
OCTOBER 31ST 1936

The wind howled outside, banging and rattling the shutters around the castle. Agnes and Irene, two young women who were a long way from home, exchanged nervous glances. Irene shivered, though whether from cold or fright she wasn't sure. She pulled her shawl closer.

"I can't see him yet," said Agnes, peering through the shutters.

"It is not yet time," replied Charika, their Indian companion.

The rain, which had stopped, started again with renewed force. It was clear to both girls that a major storm was brewing. The sound of the storm was deafening, although occasionally Irene and Agnes could hear the rhythmic chanting of the holy men from the depths of the castle.

"When will it...happen?" Agnes asked.

"Hush, child," said Charika. "In India, one must learn patience. It will happen when it is time for it to happen; not before, and not after."

Another gust of wind rattled the shutters. The candle guttered briefly, and went out.

"Where's the tinderbox?" asked Irene plaintively. "And where are the servants?"

"Hush, girl," said Charika again. "They are all busy with the preparations – with the ritual. There are no servants tonight. Tonight, we are alone."

Alone, thought Irene. Oh, how I would like to be alone once again...And into her mind floated a picture of her parents' house, her childhood home in Scotland. She felt suddenly homesick – for the gulls, the mists, the heather, and the soft fine rain that fell in the autumn. Not like this monsoon – sharp torrents and heavenly outpourings – but gentle, soothing wetness.

The chanting below became more urgent. Irene glanced at her watch. It was nearly midnight. It won't be long now, she thought.

Agnes pushed to the window again.

"Oh, I can see quite well now," she said. "There's a gap in the clouds, and the moon is out."

A gong sounded abruptly.

"Now; it is time," said Charika. She stood, a small, sprightly woman of fifty or so.

"Come," she said to Irene, and beckoned her to the window.

Irene looked across at the turrets opposite, and then down into the courtyard. Agnes was right, she thought, you could see quite well. The rain had stopped temporarily, the wind had eased, and the moon shone onto the scene below.

A large group of men were gathered in the castle courtyard. As Irene watched, the gong sounded again, and the crowd parted. Irene caught her breath as she glimpsed Ruhal – her very own prince, her husband-to-be – in the centre. He was dressed, from head to foot, in a tiger skin. As Irene watched, the men formed a circle around him and began to chant.

Ruhal began to turn on his heel, and walked backwards, slowly at first, then more quickly, inside the circle. Someone grabbed his arms and began to swing him around faster, while the chanting continued, and rose to a crescendo. He stumbled dizzily, and Irene noticed that he was blindfolded.

There was the sound of a flint striking behind her, and Irene turned to see Charika light a lantern – Irene's lantern. It threw a calm glow across the room, and Irene began to relax slightly. This is an odd way to spend the eve of my wedding, she thought. Indeed, it was a very strange wedding indeed, here in the middle of Kimbustan – a remote kingdom in India – to a Kimbustani Prince.

Irene smiled as she thought of the fortune-teller Agnes had taken her to, in Delhi, soon after she arrived. The old woman had looked Irene up and down, and without ceremony, indeed without the aid of any external apparatus at all, had announced that Irene should expect to marry a wealthy man in India in the next six months.

Agnes had looked aghast; but Irene had laughed.

"I don't know any Indian men, let alone any wealthy ones, and I don't intend to get married here. I shall be going back to Scotland in a few months," she said.

The fortune-teller looked directly at her then, her sharp eyes piercing, searching, and knowing. Irene had suddenly felt strangely uncomfortable in her gaze.

"And so you shall," the fortune-teller had said.

And that was all.

The gong sounded yet again, and the men in the courtyard led the prince to the foot of the stairs which rose to the battlements above. He stood for a moment, tall and proud, and then began the long climb towards the turrets.

"He must climb to the top," said Charika, "proclaim the incantations, take the flag, and return to the courtyard."

"Not so difficult," said Agnes.

"He is blindfolded," said Charika. "And the climb is steep."

Irene's eyes followed the route that Ruhal was taking. The steps led to a flat path along the top of the battlements, which ended abruptly at the base of a high turret. Iron rings were fixed into the wall of the turret. At the top was a hemispherical, highly polished and very slippery copper dome. A flagpole was set into the top of the dome and the Kimbustani flag could be seen fluttering dimly in the darkness. A difficult climb at the best of times; but blindfolded, thought Irene, it was a truly worthy test.

"All the Princes of Kimbustan make this climb before they marry," said Charika, in a low voice. "It is our tradition."

Ruhal reached the top of the steps, and began the traverse across the battlements. The path was narrow, with no railing to hold. Ruhal felt cautiously with his feet before each step.

"Of course," said Charika, "it is the first time a Kimbustani Prince has seen fit to marry a foreigner - even one as beautiful as you."

She gazed directly at Irene. "It is perhaps why the gods show their displeasure tonight..."

Irene gasped, and her hand flew to the amulet around her neck.

"Charika," said Agnes, "you don't believe that - do you?"

A flash of lightening split the sky. Charika turned to the window.

"The storm…is returning…" she said slowly.

It was true. The rain, which had eased off, returned in force. Within a few seconds the lashing rain had reduced the visibility across the courtyard, so that the figure of Ruhal, now at the base of the turret, was just a blur.

"Ruhal loves me," said Irene quietly. "At the tiger hunt–"

Charika turned, her figure silhouetted at the window.

"This is a land of illusion, and tricks of the light," she said. "Remember this: in India, nothing is quite as it seems. Nothing," she added fiercely.

Irene thought back to the tiger hunt, to the night when Ruhal had first taken her in his arms. That was when he had given her the lantern. It was an old, rusty thing, but valuable, he said. She had laughed, not believing him. But there could be no doubt about last night's gifts. It was a dowry fit for a princess; emeralds, rubies, gold, silver, diamonds…And then later, after dinner, he had given her something very special: the jade amulet, with its exquisite carving of a Kimbustani tiger...

"Ruhal loves me," she said again, loudly this time. "And I love him..."

A peal of thunder almost drowned out her words, and another gust of wind blew out the lantern. Irene joined Agnes and Charika at the window.

Ruhal was near the top of the turret now, although with the blinding rain it was hard to see clearly. Irene watched as he reached for the handholds set into the copper dome capping the turret. There was another flash of lightning and a peal of thunder, very close together this time.

"The storm is at its height," said Charika, quietly.

Clouds obscured the moon and Irene was grateful for the flashes of lightning, between which was inky blackness. In the next flash, Ruhal appeared to be almost at the top of the dome, and Irene saw him reaching for the flag.

Then a brilliant flash lit the sky; Agnes gasped, and Irene screamed.

The roof opposite was empty.

PART ONE

"Tim, Kelly! Come here please. I have something – something important – that I need to tell you..."

Tim frowned. He didn't like surprises.

And he didn't like the tone in his Mum's voice, either. It sounded odd; strained and worried.

He looked across the lawn – past Russ his dog, and his twin sister Kelly, who was sitting on the grass reading a book – to where his mother stood in the kitchen doorway.

"Tim, Kelly!" she called again.

There was nothing for it. Reluctantly, Tim climbed down from the tree house - his favourite spot in the garden - and made his way to the house. It was a hot August afternoon, a perfect day. Kelly was already sitting at the kitchen table.

"Sit down, Tim," said his mother. She looked serious. "Look, children, I'm afraid I have bad news for you. Your Great-aunt Irene has died."

Tim sat. He wondered who Great-aunt Irene was.

"Irene was your father's aunt," continued their mother. "She was an old lady; she lived on the coast of Scotland, near the sea."

"I don't remember ever hearing about her," said Kelly.

"Well, you wouldn't have," said their mother. "We didn't speak about her much. In fact, we hardly ever heard from her, let alone saw her. She lived in a big old house, on her own, up on the cliffs.

"To tell you the truth", she went on, smiling thinly, "we always thought that she was a bit...strange. Nothing you could put your finger on, really. Just...odd, that's all."

She paused, took a deep breath, and then she said:

"Anyway, the thing is, we're her only relatives. And she's left us the house in her will. So Daddy and I have decided that we are going to live there."

She stopped, and looked at both of them. Their jaws dropped.

"You mean - as a family?" asked Kelly.

Their mother nodded.

Tim felt stunned. Move? To Scotland? He couldn't believe his ears.

"No!" he said loudly.

They looked at him.

"No!" he repeated. "I'm not going! I like it here! I don't want to go to mouldy old Scotland!"

"Listen, Tim," said his mother. "I know it's a shock, but you'll love the house. It's on the cliffs, near the beach. There are ponies in the field next door. And you'll have your own

4

room - you're twelve now, and you can't share with Kelly for ever. We would have moved house anyway."

Tim looked at her, glumly. It seemed pointless to argue. He knew that his parents had made up their minds. Whatever he said, they were going to Scotland. It was just so sudden, that's what he didn't like.

But then there was something else, too.

Deep, deep down, somewhere in the darkest reaches of his soul, Tim felt something stir... something he hadn't known was there. It was as if a part of him had been in a deep sleep since... since he was born, and now it was yawning and stretching and uncoiling inside him. It was an odd and uncomfortable feeling, a strange mix of emotions. There was excitement and anticipation. There was something else though, something Tim didn't like. It was a feeling of...What was it, exactly? Yes - it was danger - of great danger...

And if he listened very carefully, Tim could imagine a tiny voice inside his head - a voice whispering quietly: *"Don't go...don't go to Scotland..."*

Tim took a deep breath, and shook his head. He pushed this strange feeling away, back down inside him.

He looked up at his mother's face and knew he was defeated. He would have to go. He swallowed hard, and sighed.

"Can Russ come?" he asked.

*

"It's not fair; it just isn't fair," said Tim angrily.

He was sitting with Kelly in their tree house, later that

day. On the floor were a plate of biscuits and two cans of fizzy drink.

"I know it's not fair," said Kelly. "But we'll just have to make the best of it, Tim. At least we'll all be together - our family, I mean - and I suppose in time we'll settle down in Scotland. In a way, it's rather exciting, don't you think?"

"No," said Tim shortly. "I don't."

"Look - it can't be that bad, can it? It's probably a really nice place. Mum said that we could bring our bikes. We'll be able to go out exploring. I'd love an adventure, wouldn't you?"

Tim stared at his sister. He wondered if she'd had the same strange feeling of excitement and danger that had come over him. But now the feeling had gone completely, and he was thinking again about being uprooted and moved.

"Huh!" he said scornfully.

Sometimes, he thought, Kelly said the daftest things. Adventures! What adventures were they likely to have, stuck all alone in some stupid old Scottish village?

Kelly looked at Tim. She knew what he was thinking and always had done, without having to ask. That was one advantage of being twins. Tim could be really stubborn sometimes, she thought. Couldn't he see that they really didn't have any choice in the matter? Their parents had decided what was to happen - and that was that. They'd just have to make the best of it.

Actually, it was probably Dad who had decided to uproot the family, thought Kelly. Dad was a writer. He wrote long philosophical books and articles about nothing in particular, as far as Tim and Kelly could tell, and he worked at home. He liked peace and quiet, and hated interruptions to his work.

As a philosopher, Dad believed fully in the principles of family democracy - or so he said. Yet he would often make decisions like this without asking anyone else in the family for their opinion. Kelly suspected that their mother, too, was unhappy about moving; but if so, she wasn't letting on to them.

Kelly sighed. It's funny being a twin, she thought. It's like being only half a person - or being two people at once. They weren't identical or anything - she and Tim were girl and boy for a start - and in some ways they were quite different. Tim was good at sport. He was a good swimmer, and in the cross-country running team at school. Kelly hated the water and had no interest in running around getting muddy and wet on a freezing cold day.

But Kelly was the more sociable of the two. She enjoyed singing and acting and had been in all the plays at their school. She was also more level-headed and sensible than Tim - at least most of the time.

Still, being a twin was different from being a normal brother and sister. There was a sort of invisible bond between them - almost telepathic - and Kelly could often close her eyes when she was alone and know exactly where Tim was, what he was doing, and how he was feeling. She knew Tim could do the same. Kelly had felt a sudden twinge of uneasiness when their mother had told them that they would be moving. Yet the feeling had disappeared as quickly as it had come, and now Kelly was quite looking forward to the idea.

Kelly lifted her head and looked at Tim. Their eyes met and she smiled.

Let's make the best of it. Let's have - oh, I'm going to say it - let's have fun and adventures, up there in Scotland!"

*

The removal men cheered them up with jokes and stories as they packed, but during the long drive up to Scotland, Tim felt a cloud of depression settle over him. Russ, who was sitting between Tim and Kelly on the back seat, tried to lick Tim, but he pushed Russ away and the dog eventually settled down to sleep.

Kelly tried to get Dad to tell them about Aunt Irene.

"I can't really tell you much about her," said Dad. "Some people thought she was a bit soft in the head, but I never did. As far as I know, she grew up in Scotland, but when she left school she travelled out east - to India, I think. I didn't know her very well - and she'd done all the travelling before I was born.

"When she came back home to Scotland, she never left her home again - not even to visit us down south, although I invited her once or twice for Christmas, things like that. I think maybe she'd had something of a scary time on her journey. Some of what I heard was quite hair-raising."

"I have a picture of her here," said Mum, interrupting.

She turned around in the front seat, and passed over a small photograph. It showed a plain, elderly woman, dressed in sensible country clothes. She was gazing directly at the camera, with a rather dour expression on her face, as if wishing it wasn't there.

"It's odd, having an aunt we didn't know about", said Tim. "Didn't she ever get married, Dad?"

"Oh no," said Dad. "Although..."

"What?" said Kelly, eagerly.

"I do vaguely remember hearing something," said Dad, "something about... falling in love, and a foreign Prince, I think... but I can't say I remember any details. It all sounded most unlikely to me... Hey," he said, changing the subject, "who wants to be the first to ride the ponies?"

*

The house was big and old, perched on the cliff tops overlooking the sea. Their first impression was of high, gabled windows, a steeply sloping roof, and dark grey shutters, which gave the house a feeling of brooding disquiet.

Dad parked the car on the gravelled drive, then, together, they walked up the steps onto the front porch and rang the bell.

"Mrs Rabb should be here to let us in," Dad said. Then, seeing their puzzled faces he added, "Mrs Rabb was Aunt Irene's housekeeper for many years."

They waited a moment, but the house remained silent.

"All right. We'll try the side door," said Dad.

They followed a path around the side of the house, past

the kitchen door, which was locked, and at length into an enormous garden. In the distance, Tim could see an orchard, a fishpond, and a summerhouse.

"Hey! This is open!" called Kelly.

She was standing by some French windows which were unlocked. They opened into a large room, furnished with an old carved wooden sideboard, some chairs, and – somewhat eerily – a gently ticking grandfather clock. There was a fireplace with a wooden mantelpiece, on which stood various ornaments, including an attractive, beautifully carved sandalwood box. A painting of a seated Buddha hung on the wall.

From this room, a door led into a hallway containing more wooden furniture - an occasional table, some potted plants. On one wall hung a portrait of a tall handsome man, brown skinned, wearing a turban and a white tunic. One foot rested on a tiger-skin rug. The floor of the hallway was wooden, but in the centre was a beautiful tiger-skin rug, identical to that in the portrait.

Before they could say anything, footsteps sounded on the drive outside. A moment later the front door opened, revealing a small, plain woman in her late sixties, her hair in a bun, wearing a blue checked pinafore.

"Well!" she cried, in a soft Scottish accent. "You've beaten me to it! I'm Mrs Rabb, now let's put the kettle on and have a nice cup of tea. I took the liberty," she continued, "of buying a few bits and pieces you might need. If you look in the kitchen you'll find eggs, milk, bacon, butter, cheese, cereals, bread, tea, coffee, and a few salad vegetables. Also biscuits, sugar, ham, tuna, potatoes, and one or two other things besides - I hope that's alright with you, Ma'am," she said, turning to Mum.

Mum looked a trifle pink.

"Well, er, thank you, Mrs Rabb," she said.

Mrs Rabb gave a hoot of laughter.

"Och," she said, "it's good to have some young folks living here, I can tell you! Now why don't you look around the house, whilst I make you your tea? You must all be right starving hungry now - it's a long drive up from England, that's for sure. Have a good look around. This is your new home, and I hope you'll all be very happy here – very happy indeed!"

CHAPTER TWO

The next morning, Tim jumped out of bed as soon as he woke. It was a beautiful day, the end of August, and the sun was streaming through his bedroom window. He dressed quickly and went downstairs.

Mum, Dad, and Kelly were already eating breakfast. He could hear Mrs Rabb in the kitchen frying some eggs and bacon.

Dad had been opening the morning post. Now, they heard a gasp.

"Wow!" he said.

He was staring at the letter in his hand.

"What is it?" asked Mum.

"What's wrong, Dad?" asked Tim and Kelly together.

Dad looked up. He'd gone pale. In fact, he looked as if he'd seen a ghost.

"It's a letter from Aunt Irene's solicitors," he said. "About her will. Apparently..."

He swallowed, hard. "Apparently, she's left everything to Tim and Kelly!"

Tim and Kelly looked at each other.

"What, you mean this house?" asked Kelly.

"Well, not the house," said Dad. "That was left to me, as her only nephew. No, it's everything else. She had some savings, some money in the bank, that sort of thing."

"Wow!" said Tim. "We're rich!"

"Sorry," said Dad. "I'm afraid not. There's not a lot of cash, and what there is will be put into a trust until you're both grown-up. That means that Mum and I will look after it for you for the time being."

"Oh," said Kelly, disappointed.

"Didn't she leave anything else for us?" asked Tim.

"Yes," said Dad. "She's left a few bits and pieces. You are to have that tiger-skin rug in the hallway, for example, and Kelly is to have what Aunt Irene calls her amulet, although I don't know what or where that is right now. Kelly also gets that odd picture of the Indian chap in the hall, and you get her grandfather clock."

"That's it?" asked Kelly.

"That's it," said Dad, "except..."

"Except what?" asked Tim and Kelly together.

Dad looked shifty and uncomfortable. He looked down at the table.

"I think you should tell them," said Mum. Mum had been reading the letter, and was now pouring herself a cup of coffee. She looked firmly at Dad.

"Oh, all right," said Dad. He took a deep breath.

"Children, Aunt Irene was, as you know, a little confused. She told her lawyers that she's left you all her treasure, so they put that in her will."

"Treasure?" said Tim, wide-eyed.

He stared at Kelly. She stared back.

"That's the thing," said Dad. "She didn't *have* any treasure. All she had was a small amount of money, this house, and a bit of furniture. Perhaps she imagined that she had some jewels, or something - but of course, she didn't, or we'd have heard all about it by now. Her lawyer, who looked after her financial affairs, has written to say that he doesn't know of any treasure, but apparently Aunt Irene was very insistent, so he eventually followed her instructions and included it in her will."

Tim sighed. Kelly looked disappointed.

"Look, children," said Mum who had been listening. "Be pleased with what you've got, and don't worry about this imaginary treasure. Now, it's a fine morning. Why don't we ask Mrs Rabb for a picnic, and you can do some exploring before lunch?"

*

Later that morning, Tim and Kelly explored the house and garden.

The house, at first sight forbidding, proved on closer inspection to be quite charming. Light, airy rooms, a kitchen with, as their mother said, "possibilities", a playroom, and best of all, a cellar. This was discovered by accident by Tim, who noticed some half-hidden steps near the kitchen door. He tiptoed down and saw that the cellar was damp, dark, cold and creepy. Before they could explore it though, Dad said that it would make a great wine store; and that the kids were not to play down there, especially not alone.

Tim's bedroom was near the top of the house. It over-looked the garden, and was at the end of a long passageway. Tim, who wasn't used to sleeping on his own, liked to sleep with the electric light on. Kelly's room was much closer to their parents' bedroom, on the floor below. She had a marvellous view of the cliffs and the sea from her window. Both bedrooms were large, with high ceilings, washbasins, and old wardrobes.

The garden contained various items of interest. A sundial was to be found on the front lawn. An old, long-disused children's swing was tucked away past the orchard. In the remains of what had once been a vegetable garden, the children discovered an ancient and somewhat sleepy-looking tortoise, whom they immediately named Hector. There was also a large garden shed.

They could reach the beach in two ways. At low tide, a path descended directly from the end of the orchard, quite near the house, winding down the steep cliffs to the beach below. Their father, to their immense disgust, promptly forbade them to use the path, saying that the steps were unsafe and they might fall.

The other way to the beach was by road. This was much longer, but they were able to go by bike, cycling past several cottages on the outskirts of the nearby village, past the village church and school, and over a small bridge before finally reaching the beach. It was late in the summer season and most of the tourists had already gone home. Tim and Kelly spent many hours on the beach the first few days after they arrived, exploring rock pools, paddling and swimming, or simply watching Russ chase the seagulls.

The village itself contained very little. There was a high street, of sorts, leading down towards the sea, lined with small grey-stone houses and a few shops. There was a newsagent's, a fish and chip shop, a Chinese takeaway, and a corner village shop and a sort of grocers-cum-sub-post-office. There were also two pubs, and a filling station on the edge of town. The old stone church stood just off the high street.

Very few people ever seemed to be about in the village; but those that were eyed the children with suspicion. Tim and Kelly were in the village shop one day, on an errand for their mother, and felt the eyes of the other customers upon them as they queued at the counter to pay for their purchases. Nobody spoke much. The woman behind the counter, sharp-eyed and unsmiling, took their money and then watched silently as they packed their own purchases into a plastic bag. Tim felt the back of his neck go red. As they left, he heard one of the other customers say, in a low voice, "Bloody English - up here to take our houses - and our jobs!"

Outside the shop, a boy about their own age was bending over their bikes, something in his hand. Tim had a suspicion that he'd been loitering and had seen them go into the shop.

As they approached, he straightened up and looked them full in the face, insolently. Then he turned on his heel and sauntered away up the street whistling.

As Tim put the groceries into his saddlebag, he noticed that his front tyre had been let down.

*

One afternoon, about a week after they moved, the twins were eating tea in the kitchen. Mrs Rabb had cooked macaroni cheese and made a salad. Their mother had announced that she was going to clear out the attic, and that the twins could "look after themselves, couldn't they?"

Just as they finished tea their mother re-emerged, carrying a collection of bric-a-brac - no doubt, by the sight of it, destined for the nearest charity shop or jumble sale.

"Well!" she said, putting the box down on the kitchen table. "I think that's the last of it. I don't think I've ever seen so much junk. It was all packed up in old chests and trunks, in the attic. Aunt Irene couldn't have ever thrown anything away."

"Mum," said Kelly, who thought about such things. "What are we going to do about school?"

Tim glared at Kelly. Mum smiled at her.

"You start school on Monday," she said. "Your father arranged it this afternoon. You'll go to the local school in the village for now."

Tim groaned. School - so soon! He had been hoping for at least another two weeks holiday.

Kelly looked anxious.

"I – I hope we have a nice teacher," she said, uncertainly.

"Oh, Kelly, of course you will," said Mum. "Now, we'll have to be very busy the rest of the week. I've new school uniforms to get, pens, pencils, books – a whole long list."

She picked up the box – and then put it down again, and looked at Tim.

"Here, Tim – I nearly forgot," she said.

From the box, she pulled out what looked to Tim like an old oil lamp.

"Aunt Irene left this for you in her will," she said. "Why, I've no idea, but she did. Here, take it, and give it a clean – it's covered with dust, like the rest of this junk."

Tim picked up the lamp – or lantern. Kelly looked at it enviously.

"It looks like one of those old oil lamps you see in fairy tales," she said.

Tim, not really listening to his sister, was rubbing the lantern with a damp cloth.

"Huh!" he said. "Another thing to keep clean."

"You can keep it in your room," his mother said.

So later, Tim took it up to his room, put it on his desk and, thinking about school, left it there. If he was going to start school the following week, he wanted to get in as much time on the beach as he could.

MRS. RABB

"Mrs Rabb," said Tim the following morning, as Mrs Rabb was clearing away the breakfast things. "What was Aunt Irene like?"

Mrs Rabb put down her dishcloth, and took a deep breath. She loved a good gossip.

"Well now," she said. "Most people in the village thought she probably had a screw or two loose, if you know what I mean. Not that many people knew her, of course. I knew her better than most, I reckon. No, people generally thought that she was a real recluse – mysterious and eccentric."

"Mysterious?" said Tim. "But, why?"

"Well," said Mrs Rabb, "I suppose it's because she kept herself to herself. She lived here for fifty years or more, and I've been cleaning for her for most of them. In all those years, I doubt she went down to the village more than a dozen times. She used to stay in the house – in her room, more often than not. Of course people round here used to think that because she was a recluse, she must also have been really rich. Everyone in the village used to say that she'd come back from India with pots of money - and not just money either. They thought she had jewels and gold and that sort of thing.

"You know, she'd done a lot of travelling when she was young and judging by the stories she told, she had quite a few adventures. She didn't talk much about them, but those times she did talk, when I was on my tea break an' all, she really went on. I think she probably got 'erself into quite a bit of hot water over the years."

"Of course," Mrs Rabb continued, a gleam in her eye, "not all of what she told me was fit for young ears such as yours."

"Wow!" said Tim. "Mrs Rabb, what sort of adventures did she have?"

Mrs Rabb paused, dishcloth in the air, and leant forwards confidentially.

"Well," she said. "She told me once about a tiger hunt. She'd been invited on it but she didn't want to go because she felt sorry for the poor tigers. But the person who invited her insisted, so in the end she said she would go. They all rode on elephants, and they sent beaters off into the forest. The beater's job was to make a lot of noise, and get the tiger to run towards the elephants. Then they'd shoot him, see?

"Well, your aunt was up on the top of one of the elephants when she saw the tiger on the edge of the jungle. She was the first to see it and she knew that a moment later, the others would spot it and then it would be shot."

"So what did she do?" asked Tim, his eyes round.

"She jumped from the elephant," said Mrs Rabb with great gusto, "and ran towards the tiger, shouting her head off!"

"Goodness!" said Tim. "But, wasn't she scared?"

"Och, I've really no idea," said Mrs Rabb. "Anyway, it did the trick. The tiger turned and ran. It escaped back into the jungle and everybody else was very annoyed."

"Gosh," said Tim, "what an adventure! I would have loved to meet her."

"Thing is, towards her later years, people said that she'd gone, well, not quite right in the head," said Mrs Rabb. "She started going for long walks, talking to herself all the time. No one else in the village would go near her, except me, and that's only because I was used to her little ways."

Mrs Rabb sighed loudly. "That's the trouble with all that travelling in foreign lands and hot climates, I suppose. Turns the head and addles the brain."

"Mrs Rabb," said Tim thoughtfully, "who invited her on that tiger hunt?"

Mrs Rabb looked up sharply. "Why, the Prince, of course. Prince Ruhal Maharishi. His picture's on the wall in the hallway. Now," she said, straightening up, "I must get those dishes done, or your Mum will have kittens. That's enough questions for one day. Run along now, there's a dear."

*

School on Monday morning was awful.

Tim and Kelly felt the other kids staring as they walked into the classroom together. One boy, small, with fair hair, pulled a face at Tim as he passed. Sitting next to him was the boy who'd let down Tim's tyres. Tim felt their hostile gazes on his back, as they walked uncertainly to the front of the class.

Their teacher, already in the room, inhibited any untoward behaviour from the other kids; but both twins saw and felt their hostile glances and heard their whispered comments to each other. They looked around, not knowing what to do or where to sit.

"Come here, if you please!"

They turned to face their teacher. Kelly's first thought was how old she was. Tim thought how ugly she looked. Tall, thin, and dressed entirely in black with a pointed nose and sparkling dark eyes, she fixed the children with a penetrating look as they approached. Tim felt almost as if he were being x-rayed.

"You must be Tim and Kelly McTavish. Sit there, please."

She pointed to two empty seats in the front row of the class.

As they sat, wordlessly, she continued, in a deep clear voice of total command: "I am Miss Moondancer. I have only three rules in my class. You don't talk, you do exactly as you're told, and you're never late. Obey those rules and you'll stay out of trouble. Do you have any questions?"

Tim plucked up his courage.

"What... what happens if we break the rules?" he asked.

There was a titter from the seats behind him.

"*No one* in my class breaks those rules," said Miss Moondancer, in a tone of such finality that Tim did not dare to ask anything else. "Now class, please open your English grammar books at page forty-nine and let us begin exercise seventeen."

For the rest of the morning Tim and Kelly wrestled with unfamiliar problems in strange Scottish textbooks, in a damp, dark classroom. At lunchtime they queued up obediently for food, ate quickly, and wandered out into the playground.

The small, fair-haired boy - the one who'd pulled a face at Tim - ran up to them.

"Och! So you're living at the loony lady's house," he said, by way of greeting.

"She wasn't a loony lady," said Tim indignantly.

"How would *you* know?" said the boy. "By the way," he added, not unkindly, "my name's Stewart. How d'ye like Miss Moondancer?"

"She, er...seems rather fierce," said Kelly, considering.

"Well of course, that's because of her occupation," said Stewart.

He grinned at them.

"What - teacher you mean?" asked Kelly.

Stewart laughed; but his eyes weren't smiling.

"Could you not tell?" he asked. "Teacher she may be, but she's also something else. She's a witch!"

Tim and Kelly stared at Stewart. He stared back.

"You don't believe me?" he asked. "You'll see her, now and again, a-riding around on her broomstick. She's harmless, though," he said, his mouth breaking out in a big grin. "She's not bad, even if she is a witch."

Kelly found her voice.

"I don't believe you," she said. "You're making it up!"

Stewart grinned at her. "You take a look at her cottage," he said. "It's the last in the village, near the beach. Then tell me you don't believe me."

"Stewart! Come on; football!"

The voices floated towards them from the other side of the playground.

They looked around as the other boy - Conall - pushed his way towards them, his eyes burning. Conall looked right at them.

"And you two can't play," he said to Tim and Kelly. "It's football for Scots only - not you English creeps."

He turned on his heel, and walked away.

*

"School will get better," said Dad. "It's just a question of getting used to new people and new things."

"But our teacher's so creepy," complained Kelly. "The other kids think she's a witch."

Dad looked surprised. Then he smiled.

"It sounds like your new friends have good imaginations," he said.

"They're not our friends," said Tim. "And Miss Moondancer looks exactly like a witch."

"Did you say Miss Moondancer?" asked Dad. "Well,

that's an interesting coincidence. Agnes Moondancer was your Aunt Irene's friend and travelling companion, you know, all those years ago. They were out in India together. I must look in and say hello. Now, kids, it's time for bed."

Tim went to his room. As he undressed his eye caught sight of the lantern his aunt had given him.

Mum popped in to say goodnight.

"Mum, you know I sleep with the light on?" asked Tim. "Could I try the lantern instead?"

"Of course," said Mum, and they went downstairs whilst she showed Tim how to use the oil lamp.

"You fill the bottom part with oil," she said in the kitchen. "Any oil will do. Then make sure the wick is dipping in the oil, and light it with a match."

"Easy," said Tim, as the lamp blazed into life. The flame flickered and the lamp gave off a subdued hissing and gurgling sound.

He picked the lamp up by its carrying handle, and slowly climbed the stairs to his room. The lamp threw strange shadows on the walls, giving the room a different, softer aspect. Tired from his day at school, Tim got quickly into bed.

As he drifted off to sleep he thought the hissing, gurgling sound of the lamp got a little louder and the shadows appeared to dance on the walls, faster and faster. It seemed to Tim that he could hear music in the distance, the slow rhythmic sounds of the Indian sitar, rising and falling softly. He imagined he could smell jasmine and incense.

He felt drowsy. His bedroom faded around him. Now

he saw bright moonlight. The air felt strangely warm... not like Scotland at all. He seemed to be...where? He wasn't sure but it seemed like...could it be...lying by a campfire, at night? Above him the stars twinkled in the sky - behind him he could hear the low chatter of the jungle...

Tim closed his eyes and fell asleep.

He wasn't in the jungle now. He was flying, high over the clouds, air rushing past him...

He began to slow, realising that he was suspended in mid-air...

Then he began to fall, faster and faster. The earth rushed up towards him.

Tim cried out involuntarily. He was going to die!

The scene changed. Now he was on an old-fashioned sailing ship, somewhere at sea.

Another ship, a pirate ship, was tethered alongside and pirates were swarming aboard.

A battle was raging around him, pirates against sailors...

A young boy around Tim's age ran by him, desperately trying to get to safety. A swarthy, rough-looking pirate reached out and grabbed the boy by the hair. The pirate laughed a deep belly laugh. He took out a knife and held it to the boy's throat.

The boy squealed, clearly terrified out of his wits. The pirate laughed again, his eyes burning with malice and cruelty. He called out across the deck to the most evil looking man Tim had ever seen.

"Captain, what d'yer fancy? Shall I slice his throat? Or throttle 'im? Or—"

Tim was terrified himself, terrified that the pirate would come after him next. He turned and slipped down a companionway leading into the dark recesses below...

He was in a well-appointed cabin, with good furniture and books on the walls. Faintly, from above, came the screams of the injured and dying. There was the sound of sobbing close by...a girl was crying. Tim could just make out her figure in the dim light, huddled in the corner.

Before he could say anything, rough footsteps sounded in the passage outside.

The girl stood suddenly, galvanised into action. She crossed rapidly to a low table by the doorway and struck a flint. A lantern fizzled into life...Tim gazed, his eyes suddenly wide. It was his lantern, he was sure of it!

The girl grabbed an old-fashioned but deadly-looking gun standing in the corner. Slowly, she raised the barrel and pointed it at the door. Her tears were gone now, but she was shaking all over like a leaf.

Suddenly the door was flung open to reveal the pirate chief - the same evil-looking man that Tim had seen on the deck. He held a cutlass in one hand and a pistol in the other. His coat was smeared in something sticky and bright red that could only be blood.

The pirate smiled crookedly and advanced towards the girl who backed away in fear, her trembling finger tightening on the trigger...

But the scene around Tim faded, and changed once more.

He was back in the jungle. It felt warm and peaceful,

with a scent of wild flowers and the low murmur of running water. A bird cooed softly somewhere nearby. The moon shone brightly overhead.

But there was something terribly, terrifyingly wrong...

There were eyes watching him...

Tim could feel them, just off to the right. He turned slowly, imperceptibly...Yes! Two bright eyes, staring at him, never blinking...

Who...or what...were they?

And then the scene faded again. Tim rolled over in his sleep, drifting down into oblivion, whilst his dream began to diffuse and melt into Tim's unconscious brain. In the morning he couldn't recall it at all.

Chapter Four

The following morning, the weather had changed. Outside the hills were misty and a soft drizzle fell. It was early October. Summer had gone and winter was on its way.

Kelly and Tim cycled to school along the same road that led to the beach. As they approached the first cottage - their teacher's - Tim drew in his breath, sharply. A large black cat with green eyes and white whiskers stood on the porch steps, its back arched, hissing at them. Leaning against the porch stood a wooden broomstick. The children pedalled quickly on to school in silence.

"Now, class." Miss Moondancer's voice, commanding as always, cut through Tim's thoughts. "Today, we will start our project for the term. The subject," she paused, "will be witches and ghosts."

The class was silent.

"You will do your own research for this project," Miss Moondancer continued. "For Halloween, you will dress up as a witch, ghost, goblin, or spirit, and as part of your project you will write down your experiences."

"But, Miss Moondancer," Stewart burst out, "I've dressed up on Halloween before and gone trick-or-treating. All that happens is that we get a few mouldy sweets. It's not spooky - not scary at all."

"This Halloween... will be different," Miss Moondancer said slowly in a low voice. "You will see. Now, get out your French books and turn to chapter twelve."

*

Stewart came up to Tim and Kelly at break time.

"She's quite loopy," he said. "Ghosts and Halloween! Every year, she says the same - and gives us the same project. We've been doing it since we were five! She's completely barmy. Still," he went on, "at least all we have to do is draw some silly pictures of ghosts and witches, an' write a bit - it don't take long."

Kelly said, "Don't you complain that it's always the same project?"

"Nah," said Stewart. "It's not worth it. Anyway, what d'you expect from a witch?"

*

Tim lit Aunt Irene's lamp, switched off the electric light, and climbed into bed. He felt strangely excited by Miss Moondancer's Halloween project, although he couldn't think why.

He wondered what he should dress up as. For some reason, the image of Prince Ruhal came into his mind. He found himself thinking of the tiger hunt, with the Prince and Aunt Irene sitting side by side on elephants. The lamp hissed and crackled a little, and Tim could smell and hear the sound of the jungle again, more clearly this time - the sharp tang of elephant dung, the softer musky smell of rosemary and oleander and jasmine. From far away, a parrot cooed softly. Tim could hear the elephants moving slowly through the undergrowth, and the steady sound of the beaters rattling their drums.

The lamp threw shadows on the wall. Tim could see the swaying bodies of the elephants moving through the jungle, bearers on their backs. He turned his head and thought he could make out the tiger, crouched on the edge of the jungle, watching...

*

"Dad," asked Kelly at breakfast. "Was Aunt Irene in love with Prince Ruhal?"

Dad looked a bit taken aback. "I don't really know," he said. "What makes you ask that, Kelly?"

"I think she was," said Tim unexpectedly.

"How would you know?" said Kelly, surprised.

Tim shrugged his shoulders and looked confused. He could see, clearly in his mind's eye, Aunt Irene sitting next to the Prince on the tiger hunt. He'd heard the Prince yell as she jumped from the elephant and ran to the tiger.

He had seen how they embraced when the tiger had fled and she was safe. Where these images had come from, he didn't know – but there they were, in his brain. It was all very strange indeed.

The others were staring at him now.

Tim put down his piece of toast. He wasn't hungry any more.

"I...I don't know how I know," he said quietly.

*

"Kelly," said Tim, as they cycled to school. "There's something really weird about my lamp."

Kelly wrinkled up her nose and turned her head to look at Tim.

"What d'you mean?" she asked.

Tim swallowed. He wasn't absolutely sure what he meant himself.

"It's like this," he said. "Kelly, when I sleep with that lantern on, I get strange dreams."

Kelly snorted.

"Huh," she said. "Most people put it the other way round. They sleep with the light on because they get strange dreams. Everybody gets dreams from time to time, Tim. The lantern's probably got nothing to do with it."

"No," said Tim. "It's not that. These dreams are about Aunt Irene. It's like... it's like... I'm seeing her... what happened to her. It's like *I'm there*."

Kelly looked doubtful.

"You're probably just a bit spooked out," she said. "It's all that talk of treasure and tiger hunts, and witches, and Halloween and all that sort of thing. It's just a dream you're having, that's all. It's got nothing to do with the lantern."

It was Tim's turn to look doubtful.

"Hmm..." he said. "I suppose it might be that. It just... seems so real. I can smell things, and touch things when I'm there... at least I think I can. I don't know," he sighed. "It must be a dream after all."

"Tim," said Kelly. "Do you... do you think Aunt Irene *did* have any treasure?"

Tim pushed hard on his pedals for a bit.

"Dad and Mum don't think so," he said, over his shoulder.

"The thing is," said Kelly. "Why would she make it up? About the treasure, I mean," she added.

"Dunno," said Tim. "They said she was confused."

"Mrs Rabb said she wasn't," said Kelly. "I asked her the other day, just before lunch. 'Oh no, ducky,' she said. 'Other people thought she was barmy, but she wasn't. She was bright as a button, was your Aunt Irene. Not gaga at all.'"

Tim glanced at Kelly, his eyes narrowed. "Maybe we should have a look round," he said, slowly. "Let's see if we can find this treasure."

"Yes," said Kelly. "Anyway, there's another thing. Where's my amulet, the one that Aunt Irene left me? No one says she made that up, but that's missing, so—"

35

"Maybe it's with the treasure!" said Tim.

He brightened visibly.

"Hey!" he said, "Let's invite Stewart round this weekend and have a really good search. Aunt Irene probably hid it away somewhere."

"Yup!" said Kelly. She grinned. "Also, I've got another idea. Let me try that lantern tonight. That'll prove whether it's really giving you dreams, or if it's just your imagination."

*

Kelly got into bed and switched out the light. The lantern hissed and crackled, throwing shadows on the walls. Tired from school, Kelly rolled over and fell asleep straight away.

She was drifting through the darkness, stars all around her. She felt peaceful, relaxed. Ahead of her, a light shone dimly, like the moon through clouds. Kelly felt herself drifting slowly towards it. The stars twinkled, and then began to dim. She stretched out her hand to the light...

She opened her eyes, and to her surprise saw that she was in a high-ceilinged room, with marble floors and walls. The furnishings were of old, oriental appearance. She could hear a band playing in the distance, and the sound of laughter. She was wearing a white organdie dress decorated with ribbons and lace. She had white shoes on her feet and a posy of flowers in her hand. She caught her breath. I'm... I'm dreaming, she thought – I must be.

But everything seemed very solid and real.

A pair of double doors was set into one wall. From the other side of these came the faint sounds of music and laughter. She stepped to the doors, took a deep breath, and tried the handle.

The doors opened, slowly...

She was looking into a grand ballroom, where a dance appeared to be underway. Inside, Kelly could see men and women talking, laughing and dancing. The men were in military uniform, evening dress, or Indian national dress. The women were wearing old-fashioned ballroom gowns, and most also carried posies of flowers.

A number of tables were arranged around the edge of the room, at which people were sitting. At one end of the room, a large and elaborate buffet had been set up. At the other end of the ballroom, on a raised platform, a band was playing. Indian servants, dressed in white with turbans and sashes, stood around the room at intervals, holding trays of drinks.

As Kelly watched, the dance finished. The men on the dance floor bowed to their partners, and then escorted them off the floor. One couple passed close to Kelly. The man, tall and handsome, his skin bronzed in the sun, was wearing a British Calvary officer's uniform. The girl, who somehow looked strangely familiar, was slim and attractive. Kelly stepped aside to let them pass. A card fell from the man's pocket as he passed, and she picked it up and looked at it.

It read:

The Master of ceremonies is commanded by
H.R.H Queen Shikari, and H.R.H. The Prince
Ruhal Maharishi
Of the Royal Kingdom of Kimbustan
to invite
Captain James Forlescue
of the British Calvalry Regiment
to a Dinner Dance and Ball
at the Bombay polo Club at 7.30pm on
June 30th, 1936

Kelly felt faint. What Tim had told her was true after all. She was back in India - in 1936!

She was just about to look at the invitation again when two Indian girls of about Kelly's age, also dressed in white, ran in from the corridor, talking and laughing.

"Ashwina, you cheeky thing! Papa will be furious!"

"Hush, Pari!" said the other girl. "He will not notice. And anyway, how will he know it was us?"

"Oh, he will know!" said Ashwina. "Papa notices everything. You remember when we changed the medals on his dress uniform? He should have worn his campaign medals and we switched them for Jaideep's toy ones. He noticed at once!"

"Oh, yes," giggled Pari, remembering. "And he was furious. But luckily, he's never angry for long!"

"Excuse me," said Kelly, taking a deep breath and going up to them. "Er...can you tell me where I am?"

The girls ignored her.

"Look at this," said Ashwina, reaching into her pocket and pulling out what looked like a necklace.

"Oh, it is beautiful," said Pari, reaching out for it. "Ashwina, let me try it on."

"Excuse me," said Kelly again, more loudly this time.

The girls continued to giggle and Pari began to fasten the necklace around her neck. They gave no sign of having heard her.

"Can't you hear me?" said Kelly. "What's wrong?"

Pari straightened up, the necklace gleaming in the light. As she did so, a voice rang sharply across the room, and Kelly's blood ran cold.

"Pari! Ashwina!"

Kelly looked up to see the tall figure of her teacher, Miss Moondancer, bearing down on them.

*

The person coming across the ballroom towards them looked like Miss Moondancer and sounded like Miss Moondancer, but even so, Kelly gasped in astonishment. This was a young woman, in her early twenties, not the elderly Miss Moondancer that Kelly knew.

Miss Moondancer took no notice of Kelly, but spoke directly to the two girls.

"Pari! Ashwina! It is well past your bedtime and...Pari!"

Her eyes were fixed on Pari's neck.

"Pari, that amulet belongs to your father. He has been

looking high and low for it. Take it off at once and give it to me!"

Kelly stared at the necklace – or amulet as it was, apparently – on Pari's neck. Is that mine? She wondered. But she had no time to think further, for just then, a young woman – the girl who had been dancing earlier with the British officer – came up to Miss Moondancer. She, too, was dressed in a long, old-fashioned ball gown, and was flushed in the face from her recent exertions on the dance floor. She smiled at Ashwina and Pari.

"Well!" she exclaimed, in a soft Scottish accent. "You girls look like you're enjoying yourselves!"

Kelly stared very hard at the pretty young woman, who, now that Kelly could see her close up, bore quite a resemblance to her own father...

My goodness, she thought, I do believe that this is Aunt Irene!

"Oh yes," said Agnes Moondancer to Aunt Irene, a note of sarcasm in her voice. "At least, it is clear that *certain* young people in my care have indeed been enjoying themselves. These young ladies, regrettably, have been keeping themselves amused by meddling with objects that do not concern them – and getting me into trouble by it, no doubt!"

There was steel in her voice as she turned back to the youngsters.

"Now, girls. You *will* take off that amulet, Pari, and you *will* return it to your father. You know that amulet is one of his most precious possessions, and he is most upset that it is missing. You will then both go upstairs to bed."

"Oh!" said Ashwina. "But—"

"But me no buts, Ashwina," said Agnes Moondancer, in a tone of voice that Kelly knew instantly, and which allowed no room for argument. "Go!"

The girls looked downcast; but they had to obey.

As the two girls turned to go, Kelly saw her teacher look enquiringly at Aunt Irene.

"So," said Agnes, in a more normal tone of voice, "and how are you enjoying the ball?"

Irene smiled and clasped her posy.

"Oh, Agnes," she said. "It's wonderful. The dancing is marvellous and the men are just so gallant."

"I've noticed that you've been engaged rather often on the dance floor," said Agnes, in a knowing tone and with a twinkle in her eye. "I hope you've some energy left after all those rather lively waltzes and reels."

"Why, Agnes, indeed I have," said Irene, her cheeks reddening as the gentle gibe hit home.

"I've seen you dancing with a certain captain from the cavalry, have I not? More than one dance too, I believe?"

"Why, Agnes," said Irene, smiling. "You've not been spying on me, have you?"

"Captain James Fortescue is a fine young officer, Irene, and I'm quite sure you've caught his eye. He'd make a fine match for you. Maybe you should dance with him again?"

Irene decided to change the subject.

"And how about you Agnes, have you been having a pleasant evening?"

"I have been somewhat constrained by my charges," Agnes said stiffly. "I've had to keep a close eye on those two young ladies, Ashwina and Pari, this evening. I've not had too much time for dancing."

"Och, aye," said Irene, a twinkle in her eye. "I hope you've not been too constrained to miss a dance with the Prince now, eh?"

It was Agnes' turn to redden.

"If you mean my employer," she said, stiffly, "why, no. I've not danced with him. As a matter of fact, he hasn't asked me. I imagine he has many acquaintances of higher social standing, and cannot wish to be bothered with the likes of me."

"Oh, Agnes," said Irene. "I'm sure that's not true. If the Prince were as gallant and noble as he should be, a nobleman of royal blood – if he is, then of course he would ask you to dance!"

Agnes sniffed.

"Irene, I – we – must not have ideas above our station," she said. "I am only a governess, employed to look after his daughters. And—"

"And I am only a visitor to these shores, travelling to expand my horizons before settling to a life of humdrum drudgery in the highlands of Scotland!" finished Irene, with a laugh.

Kelly had been listening to all this with interest. Now her

eye alighted on a tall, handsome Indian man on the dance floor. As the music stopped, she saw him bow to the lady he was dancing with — a fair-haired European woman — and then cross the floor towards Agnes and Irene. The woman smiled at his back, and then turned and winked broadly to her friends on the dance floor.

"Miss Moondancer!"

Agnes and Irene had their backs to him and their heads close together and had not noticed his arrival. At the sound of his voice, however, they jumped as one. Agnes turned to face him.

"Prince Ruhal!"

The Prince bowed to them. "Miss Moondancer. Are my daughters in bed?"

His voice, smooth and deep, had a strangely compelling ring to it. Kelly found herself blushing, although she was sure by now that none of them could see her.

Agnes herself had blushed scarlet. "Your highness," she said, "your daughters are indeed in bed. I will be checking on them shortly. I – I am sorry to say that they had taken the amulet, sir, but I am sure they meant no harm by it. It was a foolish, childish, prank, sir – nothing more."

"I am very pleased to hear it, Miss Moondancer," said the Prince smoothly. "The amulet is not a valuable piece of jewellery by any means, but it has been in my family for many years. It is of great sentimental value. My father gave it to me, and in time I will give it to Ashwina, my oldest child. But not yet. She is not yet...ready. Now, I hope you are enjoying the ball?"

Agnes curtseyed, and smiled at him.

"Excellent," said the Prince.

But his gaze, for the first time, rested on Irene. If Agnes had blushed pink, Irene's cheeks had become scarlet. Kelly had seen photographs of Aunt Irene as an old woman. Now she realised just how beautiful she had been - was - as a young girl. Her mouth slightly open, her fair hair framing her face, she looked almost like an angel.

"Your highness," said Agnes. "May I present my friend, Irene McTavish, on a visit from Scotland?"

The Prince did not speak. Nor did Irene. They were gazing into each other's eyes.

After a short while the Prince said, "Miss McTavish, may I?" and raised his hand. She took it, and together they stepped onto the dance floor. As the waltz began he took her in his arms, his gaze never leaving her face.

"Good grief!" Miss Moondancer muttered.

Kelly stole a glance at her teacher and saw her lips tighten, her eyes, cold and hard now, fixed on the couple on the dance floor. Abruptly, she turned and walked away, leaving Kelly alone.

*

As the music finished, Kelly saw the two leave the dance floor and sit at a table on the other side of the room. The Prince beckoned to a servant carrying a tray of cold drinks.

Kelly was enjoying herself. She was certain now that she was in a dream and invisible to everyone, but it was a very real, solid, sort of a dream, and she didn't see why she should miss out on the fun. She walked over to the buffet and helped herself to a plate of food, before going to sit near the Prince's table.

Aunt Irene and the Prince were still gazing into each other's eyes, but by now they were talking animatedly.

"Miss McTavish," the Prince was saying, "you must allow me to show you some of the sights of Bombay whilst you are here. India is a delightful country, but a young lady should be accompanied at all times. My countrymen, alas, would not consider it proper for you to wander around the city alone."

"Of course." said Irene. "I had intended to sightsee with Miss Moondancer, but—"

"Miss Moondancer is rather busy with my badly behaved daughters at present," said the Prince. "They are rather a handful, I am afraid, and she has little time off."

"Why, yes," said Irene, looking around, and failing to spot Agnes. "I wonder where she is?"

"She is no doubt settling my girls into bed for the night," said the Prince. "Miss McTavish, perhaps, if you are free tomorrow...?"

As he spoke, Kelly heard the faint tinkle of breaking glass. Oddly, no one else seemed to notice it. The Prince, indeed, had reached forward and taken Irene's hand.

"Yes...I am free," said Irene softly.

"Then let me show you the sights of the city. I will collect you at ten a.m."

Irene did not answer. She was no longer flushed. Indeed, she was rather pale, her eyes fixed on something on the other side of the ballroom.

Kelly followed Irene's gaze across the room to where a small group of older Indian women sat. One of the women had risen, and was crossing towards them. She was tall, and regal, her face expressionless. Kelly was struck by her eyes – ice black eyes, keen and piercing, like a hawk. At that precise moment they were fixed on Irene. Kelly thought that there was something vaguely, indefinably, evil about this woman – it was almost as if she weren't a human at all, but a snake, or a reptile. Her eyes were glittering and hypnotic.

Kelly felt a shiver run down her spine.

The Prince glanced up as she approached; and then turned to Irene with a smile.

"Miss McTavish, I'd like you to meet my mother, Her Royal Highness, Queen Shikari," he said.

Irene started to rise, but as she did so, the room seemed to shake. Kelly saw her Aunt curtsy to the queen, and start to speak, but things were getting blurry. The scene before her was fading, and she felt light and airy, as if she were floating away. Then she heard a voice in her ear calling her name and a hand on her shoulder shaking her awake. She opened her eyes - to find Tim leaning over her.

"Kelly! Wake up!" he said. "It's time for school, and we've had a break-in during the night. Someone's ransacked Aunt Irene's study!"

CHAPTER FIVE

"That's all?" said Stewart.

"That's all," said Kelly. "I... I was really there, Stewart. Except that they couldn't see me, but I could see and hear everything."

Stewart stared into the waves. He, Kelly, and Tim were sitting on the beach directly below the house. It was Saturday - early afternoon, a day or so after Kelly's dream.

Kelly and Tim exchanged glances. Kelly had told Tim what had happened on the way to school the previous day. They hadn't known whether it was right to tell Stewart, or not. It wasn't that they thought he might not believe them: they just felt that, as Tim put it, the lamp had been left to them for a *purpose*; and (as Kelly put it) maybe, just possibly, they would be able to use it to find the treasure - or the amulet at least. Against this background, having a third

47

person know about it seemed...wrong, somehow. And yet they had wanted to tell him, somebody or anyone: it was simply too scary a secret to keep to themselves.

Stewart lifted his head.

"Okay..." he said slowly. "Now, tell me about this break-in."

"We don't know too much about it," said Tim. "It happened on Thursday night, too - the same night as Kelly's dream. None of us heard anything, but when Mum went downstairs on Friday morning to put the kettle on, she saw the mess. Someone had broken the study window, opened it, climbed through and – this is the strange bit – started going through Aunt Irene's desk and chucking the contents all over the floor. They seemed to be looking for something."

"We called the police," said Kelly. "And they took all our fingerprints, but since nothing seemed to be missing, they weren't very hopeful that they'd find the thief.

"Someone from the village," they said.

"It'd be no one from *our* village," said Stewart sharply. "No one's that daft - or dishonest come to that. If you ask me, it's weird."

"Huh!" said Tim. "It's probably your friend, Conall, Stewart. He doesn't like us – he makes that plain enough."

"It'd not be Conall neither," said Stewart, ungrammatically. "Granted, he doesn't like you, but then you're from down south – foreigners, like."

"We're not foreigners," said Kelly indignantly. "We're English—"

"And we're Scots," said Stewart, grinning. "So you're

foreigners – up here you are. But Conall's not bad – and not daft either. I don't think he'd break into your house. No, it's a bit of a puzzle."

"We know that," said Tim, "but there is one interesting thing. Maybe, when Kelly dreamt she heard the sound of glass breaking, it was the study window being smashed."

"Yeah," said Stewart thoughtfully. "Maybe."

He stared at the waves again.

"I want to have a go with that lantern," he said abruptly.

"What?" said Kelly sharply.

"I want to try sleeping with that lantern thing on," said Stewart. "If it works as well as you say, it should be great – really exciting. Lend it to me tonight!"

Tim and Kelly exchanged glances again. Kelly shook her head.

"Sorry, Stewart," said Tim after a pause. "We can't do that. Aunt Irene left the lamp to me, and I reckon there must have been some good reason why. It's not a toy, you know. There's a reason we've got it - we just don't know what it is yet. In the meantime, I don't think we should muck about with it."

"Also," said Kelly, "you might not have any dreams at all with it. Tim's dreams really weren't very clear – he wasn't even sure what he saw. Maybe it doesn't work very well for boys—"

Stewart snorted.

"Huh!" he said. "I bet it'd work fine for me. You're just mean. You invite me over, saying we're going to have a really good look around the house for hidden treasure, but instead you drag me down to the beach and tell me some silly story about a magic lantern. And then you're too mean to let me have a go. It's not fair – really it's not."

He stood up. Tim looked at Kelly again.

"I suppose it does seem mean," he said. "Tell you what, Stewart, why don't you ask if you can stay over with us tomorrow night? Then we can all try the lantern – sleep in one room, I mean, with the lantern on. That way you'd get to try it too."

Stewart brightened.

"Yeah," he said, grinning. "OK. Sunday night. It's a deal."

Kelly looked at her watch.

"Hey, it's three-thirty," she said. "We'd better get back to the house. Miss Moondancer's coming for tea, remember?"

The boys both looked at each other, and groaned.

"Damn, I'd forgotten. Dad has these really great ideas," Tim said sarcastically, "except that they're only great for him and Mum – not us."

"Oh well," said Stewart philosophically. "If there's a *proper* visitor for tea, there's bound to be a good cake at least, and maybe scones or crumpets too."

Kelly looked up at the house above them on the cliffs.

"Come on, let's take the short cut," she said, meaning the path that zigzagged up from the beach. "It looks an easy climb."

"Nah, the rock's too crumbly," said Stewart. "Anyway, we've got our bikes here. Better go back by road."

*

"More tea, Miss Moondancer?" asked Mum.

"Why, thank you, Mrs McTavish," said Miss Moondancer, passing her cup.

Tea was nearly over. Two cakes and a plate of scones and crumpets had been demolished, mainly by Tim, Kelly and Stewart. Tim was just about to ask if he and the others could be excused – he was fed up with the formality and stiffness of the occasion and badly wanted to get on with the search for treasure – when Dad leant forward, and cleared his throat.

"Miss Moondancer," he said. "I understand that you knew my aunt Irene – travelled with her, in fact."

"Oh yes," said Miss Moondancer, putting down her cup. "I did know her. We were at school together, a boarding school near Edinburgh – that is where we met. I did not travel with her to India – I travelled to India on my own, and she came out to join me later."

"What made you go to India, Miss Moondancer?" asked Mum.

"I saw an advertisement in *The Times*," said Miss Moondancer primly, "for the position of Governess to the daughters of the Prince Ruhal Maharishi of Kimbustan. My mother and father had both died when I was young. They left me with a little money – enough to pay for my education at a private boarding school, where I met your aunt, Mr McTavish. But once I reached eighteen, our family lawyer made it clear to me that I would need to seek work.

There was not enough money left to enable me to live a life of leisure.

"I liked the idea of living abroad for a while. The post suited my talents, and since I had no family in this country I had no hesitation about applying for the position.

"I soon found that the Prince did indeed need a governess. His wife had died of the cholera some years earlier, leaving him two young daughters and a baby son – Ashwina, Pari, and Jaideep. They were wealthy – very wealthy, in fact – as I suppose you would expect. They had a large summer palace in Bombay and spent quite a lot of time there, but their main home was a castle, high up in the hills of Kimbustan, built many hundreds of years previously - when I suppose times were much more dangerous than they are today.

"The children had all the material things they wanted or needed, but, without the influence of a mother, I am sorry to say that by the time I arrived, the effects of years of indiscipline and indolence had taken their toll. The girls, who by then were ten and twelve, were rather spoiled – in fact, they badly needed taking in hand. Their father couldn't handle them and their grandmother, Queen Shikari – an evil woman if ever I met one – was a bad influence upon the children. Luckily, she spent most of her time trying to meddle in government affairs and politics, so the children didn't have too much to do with her.

"I did my best with those children. It was hard, but I was delighted that by the time Irene and I had to leave, the girls had changed from being sullen and insolent, to being pleasant, polite, and helpful – most helpful, in fact."

Tim had pricked up his ears.

"Miss Moondancer, what was the Prince like?" he asked eagerly.

Miss Moondancer sniffed.

"He was a typical male," she said. "He was very well intentioned towards his daughters, but hardly ever there – gadding about town, or at his polo club, or on hunting trips. When he was around, although he acknowledged the need for discipline – and, in fact, would always ask me to be strict with them – he himself would spoil them rotten. And of course," – Miss Moondancer sniffed again – "he certainly had an eye for the ladies, as they say. He had quite a few lady friends, which was not surprising really. He was good looking, rich and a Prince – quite a catch."

"And Aunt Irene caught him?" said Dad, smiling and raising an eyebrow.

"Yes, well, that's history now," said Miss Moondancer. "Poor Irene fell in love with him – head over heels. She met him at a dance, soon after arriving in India, and, according to her, it was love at first sight. I tried to talk her out of it, but I couldn't: she was besotted by him. They spent most of each day together in Bombay, and later in Kimbustan, the Prince's ancestral home. For a while, I hardly saw them, and neither did his daughters," she added darkly.

The room was silent now. The grandfather clock ticked softly in the hallway, and the lengthening rays of the evening sun streamed through the window onto the tea-table. Tim, Kelly, and Stewart sat entranced by the tale that was unfolding.

"He asked her to marry him one night, in the jungle," Miss Moondancer continued. "They'd been on a tiger hunt. I knew at once that she shouldn't marry him. I had heard the gossip in the palace – a governess is midway in the social order between servant and master, you know, and we often hear both sides – and I knew the opposition to the idea of a prince marrying a foreigner. The Prince's mother, Queen Shikari, was against it for a start. She hated the idea. So did most of the citizens and servants. There was only one person in the palace, beside myself, who supported the marriage, and that was Charika, the children's nurse. She was about twenty years older than Prince Ruhal, and had been his nurse when he was a baby, and later the nurse to his three children. She helped me a lot in looking after the girls and we got to know each other very well. She believed that the Prince should be free to do what he liked.

"Many people spoke to the Prince and asked him to reconsider. To everyone he gave the same answer: 'This is the woman I love. What does it matter that she is not Indian?' His mother said nothing to him, but her displeasure was plain, and she was the sort of woman used to getting her own way.

"I tried to talk to Irene many times, but she would hear nothing against the Prince. 'Agnes,' she would say, 'Why should I care if other people are opposed to our marriage? I love Ruhal, he loves me, and that is all that matters.' I tried to explain to her the difficulties she would face – that Ruhal would be an outcast, that his mother would disinherit him and that ultimately he would resent Irene for it – but she laughed. She said that I was making difficulties over nothing, and walked away, It was a very difficult time."

Miss Moondancer sighed and looked out of the window. Nobody spoke. At length she continued.

"They never did get married in the end. The Prince was killed on the eve of his wedding, in a tragic accident. So, the problem was solved."

You could have heard a pin drop in the room at that moment.

"What happened?" asked Dad, quietly.

"He fell from the roof of his castle whilst attempting a silly stunt," said Miss Moondancer. Something of her old spirit had returned now and she sniffed loudly. "A tragedy, of course, and Irene was terribly upset at the time. The best thing for her was to leave India immediately.

"So, of course, we came straight home from India, to Scotland, to this village. And I must go right now, I'm afraid. I'm expecting visitors to stay for a few days and I've many things to get ready."

She rose abruptly from the table; and suddenly, the spell was broken.

"Miss Moondancer," said Tim. "Was there, I mean, did the Prince have – did he give Aunt Irene any treasure?"

Miss Moondancer stopped and looked at Tim, her sharp eyes piercing and her expression severe.

"Master McTavish, you've been listening to too many wild stories from your housekeeper no doubt, and maybe others too," she said. "There is no treasure for you. Of that, you can be sure!"

"But—"

"But me no buts, if you please," said Miss Moondancer primly, and she turned to go.

In the hallway, she stopped and looked at them sternly.

"I hope you are all working on your Halloween project, children," she said. "It's on Tuesday night - you'll need your costumes ready for then, so don't forget."

And then she was gone.

*

After she went, Stewart turned to the others and breathed a huge sigh of relief.

"Phew," he said. "What a load of rubbish. Anyway, now that old bat's gone, let's go and do something else for a bit."

"Yeah, okay," said Kelly. "Let's play hide-and-seek in the garden. It's not dark yet and somehow I feel that after that little story, I want to run around outside..."

"You can hide first, Stewart," said Tim. "We'll count to thirty, and then come to find you."

"Okay," said Stewart, and he ran out through the French windows into the garden.

Kelly looked quizzically at Tim. He frowned.

"Well," he said. "What do you think? About the treasure, I mean. Miss Moondancer was pretty definite, and she must have known - after all, she was there."

"Look," said Kelly. "Who knows? I'm sure she didn't know everything that was going on - she only thinks she did. And what about the Prince and his strange accident? She didn't say much about how it happened, did she?"

"No," said Tim thoughtfully. Then he brightened. "Come on! It must be thirty by now. Let's go and find Stewart."

They raced into the garden, laughing and shouting. Stewart didn't seem to be in the obvious places. They checked the greenhouse, the summerhouse, behind the trees in the orchard. He wasn't there.

"He couldn't have gone home, could he?" said Tim.

"It is odd – we've looked everywhere," agreed Kelly.

Then in the distance, coming from the house, they heard a "Coo-ee!" As they ran along the pathway they could see Stewart waving and shouting to them.

"I've been hiding *ages* and you haven't found me!" he said.

"Where were you, Stewart?" asked Kelly.

Stewart pointed to an open doorway. "Down there," he said. "In the cellar."

"But that's out of bounds. We're not supposed to go down there," said Tim. "Dad's forbidden us—"

"Well, no one told *me*," said Stewart. "Come down. It's fine – unless you're scared of spiders or something?" he added, looking at Kelly.

"Oh no," said Kelly, hurriedly. "Tim's the one who doesn't like spiders. Let's go down."

The steps led down to a dark room that seemed to stretch a long way back under the house. It was dark and shadowy, giving the room a very scary feel.

"I waited near the bottom of the steps," whispered Stewart.

"But I thought that *you* might like to explore it."

"You mean, you were too scared to explore on your own," whispered Kelly.

"Nah," whispered back Stewart. "I'm not scared of anything, me. I just thought, seeing it's *your* house, you'd want to be the first to look around."

"Yeah, well, it is pretty creepy down here," said Tim. "I think we'd better get some light." He went off upstairs and after a short while came back with a battery-operated electric torch. He switched it on.

Immediately the shadows sprang back. The room was long and broad with pillars and columns supporting the house above. The ceiling and floor were uneven, giving the cellar a cave-like appearance. They walked gingerly, slowly, into the middle of the cellar, Tim shining the torch towards the further recesses.

"At least there aren't any spiders," whispered Kelly.

"Well, not many anyway," said Stewart, brushing one off his clothes.

Tim's torch had picked out an object half hidden behind one of the pillars.

"Hey, what's that?" he asked.

"That" appeared to be a long, flattish object covered in a very dirty, moth-eaten old blanket. Tim held the torch whilst Kelly and Stewart pulled the blanket away.

And then the three of them gasped as one. They had uncovered a large box, wooden with metal clasps, with some sort of ancient Indian script inscribed around the lid.

It was, undoubtedly, a treasure chest.

CHAPTER SIX

"Just our luck for the chest to be *locked*," said Tim despondently, as he sat up in bed.

"You didn't suppose Aunt Irene was going to leave her treasure chest lying about unlocked, did you?" said Kelly sarcastically.

Tim sighed.

"Well, all we have to do now is find the key," said Stewart.

"Do you have any idea how much junk there is, lying around this house?" asked Tim. "There's piles and piles and piles. My mum's started tidying up but it'll take ages for it all to be sorted."

Then a sudden thought struck him. "I say, she's been chucking some of it away. You don't suppose she could have thrown the key out, do you?"

"People don't throw keys out if they don't know what

they're for," said Stewart. "Anyway, why don't you ask her?"

"We haven't told her – them – about the treasure chest, remember?" said Tim. "We agreed we'd keep it a secret. We don't want my parents poking their noses in, so I can hardly ask Mum about a key without her wondering what on earth is going on, can I?"

It was the following evening, the Sunday of the sleepover. Tim, Kelly, and Stewart were lying in Tim's room. Tim was in his bed; Kelly and Stewart were on camp beds. Tim and Kelly's mum had reluctantly agreed to a "sleepover", but only on condition that the children were well behaved.

"We'll just have to search for the key," Kelly said. "We found the chest, didn't we? Anyway, it's just possible that we might find a clue in our dreams – wouldn't that be exciting?"

"Huh!" said Stewart. "I still think you're making all this up about the lantern. I bet I don't have any dreams. I think it's all a big trick you're playing on me."

As if on cue, Mum called from downstairs. "Children, it's bedtime. Switch the light out now and no talking."

"Well," said Tim, getting out of bed to light the lantern and switch off the electric light, "now is your chance to find out, Stewart. Here goes."

*

Stewart lay on his camp bed, staring at the ceiling. He didn't feel very sleepy, although the dim light from the lantern gave the room a pleasant feeling and created little flickering patterns on the wall. Presently, from the other beds, came the sound of steady breathing and the occasional snore. Just as I thought, he said to himself. This dream business is a waste of time. The others are fast asleep in their beds and nothing is happening.

Stewart started to relax. The lantern's flickering caused the odd shadow to fall on the ceiling, almost as if he was staring at the sky on a dark night and looking at clouds rolling across the heavens. A soft breeze blew in from the window. It seemed unusually warm for a Scottish October. Stewart turned his head slightly. He could make out the moon, large and luminous, peeping from behind the clouds. There was the soft trickle and ripple of water moving in the background and once Stewart thought he heard a bark or call from some sort of animal. The stars had come out now – the wind was blowing the clouds away. Stewart felt very calm and relaxed, but also strangely tired. He closed his eyes, rolled over, and fell into a dark, dreamless sleep.

*

Tim lay facing the bedroom wall, looking at the flickering reflections from the lamp. He wasn't sure about this dream business. Kelly seemed to have had a vivid experience, but he could only dimly recall a rather odd feeling of being somewhere else. He tried to remember exactly where. He had heard birds calling, it had been warm, and there had been a vague flickering light - a campfire perhaps.

61

Tim felt very relaxed. He wasn't sure whether he had fallen asleep but now he noticed that the flickering reflection had changed. He lifted his head and saw that the light was moonlight, reflecting on water. He was lying on soft grass by the banks of a river somewhere. He was dressed in a long white cotton shirt. The river was flowing swiftly and the other bank of the river was dense with bushes and trees.

The stars shone brightly giving enough light to see by but the sky had a luminous feel about it, as if dawn were not far away. A few clouds covered the moon, but a warm breeze was blowing them swiftly across the sky.

Tim stood up, cautiously. He found himself in a clearing by the riverbank, surrounded by trees. To the right, the river fell away steeply and Tim could see rocks and rushing water – the rapids. It felt very warm for night time and the trees and bushes had a lush, luxuriant look you didn't see in Scotland. A path led from the clearing into the trees.

Oh well, thought Tim, excited. I seem to have made it – I'm in the dream! Now, I wonder where Kelly and Stewart are?

Carefully, quietly, he began to follow the path into the jungle.

*

Kelly lay looking out of the bedroom window, at the last vestiges of the sunset as the sun went down behind the hills overlooking the house. She wasn't sure she wanted to dream again. The last one had been so vivid, so real, that it was almost frightening. But the presence of the others in the bedroom reassured her and she began to relax.

After a while she realised that, oddly, the glow behind the hills was not fading but imperceptibly brightening. The hills too, had lost their familiar look and seemed harder, steeper, sharper - more like mountains. She sat up and saw with a shock that she was no longer in Tim's bedroom at home, but instead in some sort of a hut. She was sitting on some straw matting on the floor, and had been looking out through a glassless window – just an opening in the wall, really.

I'm in the dream again, she thought, feeling a mixture of alarm and excitement. She looked down at herself. No ball gown this time. Instead, she was wearing a simple silk sari. She stood up. As far as she could see she was alone in the hut.

She pushed open the door. She was in a clearing high up in the hills, on a sort of wide ledge. Below she could see, in the distance, the broad sweep of a fast-flowing river, and rising up towards her a dense jungle. At one point along the riverbank she could see what looked like an encampment. There were tents down there, and a campfire.

There was a path leading down from the far side of the ledge, but as Kelly walked towards it, she heard the sound of low talking to her right on the edge of the ledge. It made her stop and look round.

Prince Ruhal and Aunt Irene were there, sitting on the ground behind a low bush. The Prince had his arm around Irene as they gazed at the river below and the slowly brightening dawn.

She didn't like to eavesdrop, but somehow Kelly found herself sitting on the ground next to her aunt as they whispered.

"My darling," the Prince was saying, "we've been up here on this lookout, sitting out under the stars nearly all night. Soon it will be dawn and we must go down to join the others..."

Irene sighed and snuggled closer to him. "Ruhal, I love you," she whispered.

"And I love you, Irene," replied the Prince, smiling at her. He paused. "Irene, you were so brave today – yesterday – at the tiger hunt. You could have been killed! You were so silly and yet so brave. Yesterday, as I saw you run towards that tiger, I suddenly knew, deep in my heart, just how much I loved you, and what loosing you would mean to me. Yet this morning, my darling, I find that I love you even more. I now know that I love you with all my soul; and I know also, that I will love you for ever, for all eternity. Oh, Irene, we will be together as the sun and the moon, and our love will shine over this Kingdom for all time..."

Irene giggled. "Ruhal, you don't get the sun and the moon in the sky together – even a simple girl from the Scottish highlands knows that!"

She patted Ruhal's arm affectionately.

"Look, my darling..." said Ruhal quietly.

He pointed and it was true. Although the full moon still shone brightly in the sky, the first rays of the sun were starting to peep across the land from the mountains opposite. Together, they watched as the sun started to rise.

"It's so beautiful," said Irene softly.

"I wanted you to see my kingdom for yourself," said Ruhal. "I brought you up here, Irene, so you could see its beauty and the vastness of the land. My home – my castle – lies high up in these mountains." He pointed to the snow-capped range opposite. "My kingdom stretches almost as far as you can see; and yet, nothing in India is quite as it seems. This beautiful landscape contains many things of wonder. Yet it also contains poverty, disease and starvation. The jungle, with its lovely green carpet of trees and its marvellous flowers and birds, also holds many dangers: snakes, poisonous spiders and wild animals – including that tiger we did *not* shoot yesterday..."

He gave Irene a playful pinch, and then sighed.

"There is one other carefully-crafted illusion in this kingdom," he said, his voice low and serious now. "You see, my dear, my subjects believe me to be Kimbustan's ruler, but some of us know that the real power in this kingdom rests with your people – the British. It is the British who are truly in command...

"And your fellow countrymen, Irene, are so arrogant. White people are superior to Indians – that is what they believe. Oh yes," he went on. "I know *you* don't believe that, my darling, but it is true for most of your countrymen. Listen, I will tell you a story.

"When I was eighteen, as you are, young and idealistic and perhaps a little headstrong and foolhardy, I was determined to join the British army. There is a cavalry regiment based not far from here in the plains. Of course, my family would never have allowed it, had I asked them, so I didn't ask. Nor did I apply through official channels. Instead, I dressed in Kimbustani peasant robes, and Baku, my manservant, and I rode down early one morning to their camp and applied to join the regiment."

Irene stared at him. "What happened?"

Ruhal shrugged his shoulders.

"Absolutely nothing. We weren't even allowed to enter the camp – turned away at the gate. No Indians may join the regiment – that's what we were told.

"I got over it. To tell you the truth, I don't think I would have made a good soldier. I'm not used to taking orders for a start. But Baku – he was furious. He's the best horseman in the palace, and the British wouldn't even give him a chance to show what he could do. He's not a cavalryman, of course. You can't be without training, for battle conditions are very different from regular riding; but he could have been good. He's never got over it. He hates the British now. But there was nothing we could do. The British were immovable.

"The British are in charge; they rule the roost as you British like to say, and now" – he turned to face Irene – "I can do nothing without the permission of the British high Commissioner. Of course," he added, seeing Irene's frown, "the British do their best, but what do your people really know of our ways, our customs and our beliefs? No; nothing here is quite as it seems, my darling."

"Except our love..." said Irene, gazing up at him.

"Except our love," said the Prince softly, and pulled her even closer.

They sat, quietly looking out over the broad vista of the land, as the sun rose slowly over the mountains.

"Many people have spoken to me," said the Prince, at length. "They believe I should find an Indian girl for my wife – someone from my own people. You know, Irene, that although the British have done many good things for my country – built schools, hospitals, restored the rule of law and brought peace to us – you British are not welcome here. My countrymen wish you to leave."

He sighed again. "My people are very superstitious. A foreigner in the family is not welcome to them. That is why my decision has been a hard one."

"What decision, Ruhal?" Irene said, wonderingly.

Ruhal, in time-honoured fashion, was on his knees. He had taken Irene's hand in his and was gazing into her eyes.

"Irene, I want you to be my wife..."

Irene opened her mouth to speak but Ruhal put his finger to her lips.

He paused, and then went on, "Please, do not under-estimate the difficulties you will face with my people; but Irene, please, marry me. I love you, and today I realised something tremendously important...I realised, for the first time, that I cannot live without you, Irene. Please..."

He fell onto his knees again and clasped her hands, looking up into her face. "Please Irene, say yes?"

Irene looked deep into his eyes, tears running down her face as the emotions surged within her.

"Oh Ruhal, darling Ruhal – yes!" she whispered. And they fell into each other's arms in an embrace.

After a while, Ruhal pulled himself away.

"I have something for you," he said, and reached down to a bag at his feet.

Irene was expecting a ring, but to her surprise he pulled from it what looked like an old oil lamp.

"This is almost the most precious thing I possess," he said. "I give it to you as a gift on our betrothal. It has a long history. It was made originally for a Sultan who ruled a kingdom in the Persian Gulf. He gave it to my family as a reward when one of his ships was captured by pirates in the Indian Ocean."

"It looks just like an old sort of lantern," said Irene, taking it in surprise.

"It, too... is not quite as it seems," said Ruhal. "Be careful with it, Irene. Keep it safe, my darling."

"Oh, Ruhal..." said Irene, and she put the lantern at her feet.

She turned to kiss him, at first softly, then more and still more passionately, and Kelly knew that it was time to leave them alone together.

CHAPTER SEVEN

Tim walked along the path through the jungle. Although it was still dark, there was enough light for him to pick his way. In the trees he heard the call of birdsong and the distant chatter of monkeys, just as he had in the previous dream. He shivered a little even though it was not cold, and walked a touch faster.

At length he came to a sort of gorge and he could see that here was a tributary of the main river. Water was cascading down from the hills above – melted water from the high snows probably – and it had worn a deep chasm through the rocks. Looking downstream, he could see that the tributary flowed into the main river a short distance away.

The path led to a sort of rope bridge across the gorge. It was a very simple affair: one heavy thick rope stretched across the divide for the feet, two parallel lightweight ropes for the hands to hold and some twine arranged in a v-shape to bind the whole thing together. The sides of the bridge were almost entirely open and the footing narrow; you had to put one foot in front of the other, as the single thick rope for the feet was itself only a couple of inches wide. Worse, the whole structure swayed and rocked dangerously as Tim eased across it, taking his time and holding very tight with both hands. He breathed a sigh of relief as he reached the other side.

A little further on the path rounded a bend and Tim found himself in the campsite. This was an open clearing surrounded by jungle. A number of tents were arranged around a large campfire. Some of the tents, for the Sahibs, were quite grand and were clustered together. A number of smaller tents were set up on the far side of the clearing. Tim guessed that these were for the servants. In the distance he could see elephants tethered to trees.

The first light of dawn was in the air but there was almost nobody about. Two Indian men were sitting on the far side of the campfire, talking quietly, but otherwise everyone appeared to be asleep.

Tim was about to hide in the shadows under the trees, but then he realised that, if what Kelly had told him was true, the men probably couldn't see him. He approached them cautiously.

As he got closer something strange struck him. The men were talking in Kimbustani – or so Tim supposed – but he was able to understand them.

"Just our luck," one was saying, "we have to guard the camp at night and then work all day and for what? What danger can we possibly face; what are we guarding against?"

"It is the Prince's orders," the other said. "And you know, Baku, that the royal family must be guarded at all times. Also, that tiger is still loose and in the jungle somewhere. It is angry now, and dangerous too..."

Baku spat into the fire.

"Bah," he said scornfully. "But for that *foreigner*, that Scottish woman, the tiger would be dead by now and we would be paid our bonus. You know we are only paid a pittance on these hunts. Unless we make a kill and take the pelt of the animal, our families will starve. Did she think of that when she made her noble gesture? Tarun, these British – I loathe them, I despise them and I hate them! I want to rid our country of them! Bah!"

He spat again. "I tell you, Tarun, if she becomes queen..."

"Baku, she will not become queen. I am quite sure of it," said Tarun. "The Prince would never ask a foreigner, a British foreigner, to——"

"Tarun, you are a fool!" said Baku. "Listen to me. Do you know where they are tonight? Do you think they sleep in their tents? I saw them – from the shadows, I saw them. I saw them tip-toe out of the camp, arms around each other, when they thought that we were all soundly sleeping. And Suhaila, the Queen's personal lady-in-waiting told me..."

He lowered his voice and put his mouth to Tarun's ear so that Tim could no longer hear what they were saying.

As they spoke, Tim's eyes had wandered as he became aware of the dim glow of a candle coming from one of the larger tents. He stood, and walked carefully to the entrance. Inside sat two women. Despite the early hour, both were dressed in long silk saris decorated with rich colours and patterns, and laced with gold. The older woman was speaking in a low, urgent tone. Her eyes – sharp, black and glinting – were narrowed and her face was hard. Her hand, gripping the handle of a walking stick, revealed the tenseness within her.

"My son is a fool, Suhaila," she said bitterly. "He is dazzled by her – silly, empty, thing that she is. She has turned his head and made him take leave of his senses."

The other woman was a little younger and her tone was deferential. "Your Highness," she said, "I am sure that Prince Ruhal would not—"

"Do you think I do not know my own son!" said Queen Shikari, forcefully. "He is crazy about her. He has eyes for nothing else – at present anyway. He will ask her to marry him – I know it. I saw it in his face today when that idiot girl ran at the tiger."

Her hands grasped the stick still tighter.

"Oh, how I wish that the tiger hadn't turned and run away," she said, in a low tone.

"Queen Shikari!" said Suhaila, surprised. "You don't mean..."

The queen nodded, her face hard.

"I am ashamed of myself for thinking such thoughts," she said. "I – I do not wish for her to die – not really. If only... if only she would go away and leave us in peace."

Her shoulders began to heave, and for a minute she fought to control herself. She swallowed hard. When she spoke again, it was in a low, level voice.

"Suhaila, we must make plans. We cannot delude ourselves. Ruhal is crazy about that girl. It seems to me that a wedding is almost certain. We must limit the damage that Ruhal can do to our Kingdom and our people by his foolishness.

"Suhaila, you are my most senior lady-in-waiting. Listen carefully, for this is my plan. You will travel to Delhi with two of my most trusted male servants. You will take this with you—" She went to the back of the tent and pulled out a box. "You will visit the bazaar, and..."

Her voice fell to a whisper but Tim was no longer listening.

He was staring at the box. It looked just like Aunt Irene's treasure chest.

*

Kelly walked down the path from the lookout. She wondered where Tim and Stewart were. Was she here alone?

It was peaceful, walking quietly downhill through the jungle. Kelly thought about her aunt up on the lookout with her Prince, on what was perhaps the happiest day of her life. I'm glad I've seen her, she thought. I feel that I know her now, although I haven't been able – and will never be able – to speak to her, face to face. I have a memory of her. She isn't a stranger to me.

And then Kelly thought of what was to happen in Irene's future and the feeling went through her that maybe she was glad she couldn't speak to her aunt. Because the future could not be changed and so what was to happen, had to happen. Karma, she dimly remembered: you cannot change fate.

The path approached a deep gorge, the same one seen by Tim, although she was on a different path higher up than Tim's and the bridge across was different – a suspension bridge with a slotted wooden base. Far below, the waters raged their way down to the river.

A squirrel was by the edge of the path, collecting nuts. As she approached, it turned and scuttled off into the trees. This startled Kelly, although before she could think about it she heard voices from the bridge.

"Ashwina, you bad girl!"

"Pari, come here now!"

There came the sound of giggling and Kelly realised that Ashwina and Pari were each engaged in imitating the voice of Miss Moondancer. Pari was best at it, but Ashwina was outstanding too. They were sitting on the suspension bridge itself, feet dangling over the edge, laughing and joking about their governess. Before Kelly could approach, however, they heard a voice from the pathway below.

"Ashwina! Pari! Where are you?"

"It's Miss Moondancer," said Pari in alarm. "Now we are for it!"

They scrambled to their feet but before they could run, Miss Moondancer appeared. She was wearing a light tunic and sun hat and had walked up from the camp.

"Ashwina, Pari! What *are* you doing? Don't you know it is dangerous to wander about by yourself in this jungle?

Come back down to the camp at once! What *would* your father say?"

"Oh, Miss Moondancer," began Ashwina. "It is so beautiful here in the early morning. We just wanted to take a walk before breakfast."

Miss Moondancer, surprisingly, softened a little.

"It is certainly beautiful," she replied. "This is a beautiful country, if somewhat full of surprises. However, you know that you should never go off anywhere, Ashwina, without asking me first."

"But you were asleep, Miss Moondancer, and we didn't want to wake you," said Pari. "We were doing no harm up here."

"Well, that's as maybe," said Miss Moondancer. She sniffed. "Well, I suppose there's nothing wrong with a walk before breakfast. Being in the open air certainly brings on an appetite, doesn't it?"

Miss Moondancer sat down on the bridge with the girls. They stared at the rushing water below.

"Miss Moondancer," asked Ashwina at length, "do you believe in ghosts?"

Kelly stared in surprise at the question. Miss Moondancer, however, did not bat an eyelid.

"Certainly not," she replied. "Whatever gave you that idea, Ashwina?"

"I wish our mother was a ghost," said Ashwina. "Then we should see her from time to time."

"I hardly remember her." said Pari. "Jaideep doesn't

remember her at all. I look at her picture sometimes." She sighed. "I think I miss her, but I'm not sure. She died such a long time ago now."

"I miss her," said Ashwina. "I remember her - I was five when she died, almost six."

All three of them stared silently at the water.

"Well, I suppose we'll be getting a new mother soon," said Pari, after a pause.

"Pari, what do you mean?" asked Miss Moondancer sharply.

"Miss McTavish – she is to marry our father," said Ashwina, giving a mysterious smile. "Everyone in the palace says so. It is hot gossip in the servant's quarters and the parlour maids are even making bets on which month the marriage will be."

"Ashwina, I think I would know if there was to be a marriage," said Miss Moondancer stiffly. "Miss McTavish is my friend and I think she would tell me first if she were to accept a marriage proposal."

"Well, maybe she doesn't know yet," said Pari. "But everybody else thinks she will marry our father. I don't mind though. I didn't like her at first, but then I thought about it. Miss Moondancer, I didn't like you at first, when you arrived. Everyone said you were a witch! You were so strict with us! You made us be polite when we wanted to be cheeky, quiet when we wanted to be noisy, keep our clothes clean when we wanted to be dirty – all sorts of things you make us do. But then I thought, we must have been very difficult children for you to care for, Miss Moondancer, and we made your job very hard. But we got used to you and now it's not so bad.

"I don't want a new mother. I had a mother but she's dead now, and I have a governess, but if I have to have a new mother, like Miss McTavish, I suppose I'll get used to her - just like I got used to you. Anyway," she sighed, "I don't suppose we'll see much more of her after they are married than we see of Daddy now, so it won't really make any difference, will it?"

This was such a long and surprising speech for Pari to make, and contained so many home truths, that Kelly was amazed when Miss Moondancer put her arms around the children and hugged them tightly.

They sat quietly for a while longer and then Miss Moondancer got to her feet.

"Come on, girls," she said, and her voice sounded unsteady for just a moment. "It's time to go back for breakfast."

"Miss Moondancer, are you crying?" asked Pari, looking up at her.

"Certainly not," replied Miss Moondancer briskly.

But tears glistened on the teacher's cheeks, as they turned and walked down the path together.

*

Tim was still standing by the campfire staring at the treasure chest, when he saw the three girls walking hand in hand into the camp. He realised that one of them was Miss

Moondancer. The other two must be Pari and Ashwina, the girls Kelly had told him about. Miss Moondancer paused at the entrance to the camp and her hands reached to her neck in order to remove her sun hat. A pendant round her neck glinted in the early morning sunshine.

Then Tim saw Kelly. She had followed the girls down and was standing just beyond them, half hidden on the jungle path. She waved and smiled to him, relieved that he was in the dream too.

Tim was about to call over to Kelly, confident now that neither of them could be seen or heard, when his eye was caught by a small movement in the undergrowth. He frowned. It was difficult to see in the dawn shadows, but...

He caught his breath. He could make out the outline of the tiger. It was half hidden in the jungle, crouched low, ready to spring. Miss Moondancer, Pari, and Ashwina were talking and laughing now, oblivious to the danger. Then he suddenly realised that the tiger was not looking at the three people on the path in front of him, but at—

"Kelly!" he shouted. "Run! Run now!"

He snatched up a burning stick from the campfire and hurled it at the tiger.

Kelly, startled, looked around and saw the tiger crouched in the undergrowth. She began to run. The tiger, thrown off balance by the blazing log, snarled, recovered itself, and charged after Kelly.

Tim's quick thinking had gained a few precious seconds for Kelly and she sprinted through the camp, looking desperately for safety. Her feet flew down the river path that Tim had taken, out of the camp. She knew a girl could not outrun a tiger, but maybe...

She reached the rope bridge just half a second before the tiger. She had no time to think – she threw herself over the rope railing, and down into the raging torrent below.

*

Tim reached the bend in the path, another blazing log in hand, just in time to see Kelly disappear off the bridge into the river. For a second it looked as if the tiger was about to follow but as Tim ran towards him, brandishing the log, he turned tail and disappeared into the jungle.

Tim stared over the railing. He couldn't see Kelly and he had remembered two things. One, she couldn't swim very well; and two, the rapids, which lay just below the riverbank clearing.

"Kelly!" he yelled. There was no reply.

Then he saw her, far away, head bobbing just above the surface of the water. She was being swept into the main channel of the river towards the rapids.

*

Kelly fought to keep her head above the surface of the river. She could hardly breathe, and had already swallowed a lot of water. The currents were very strong here and her skin and bones were bruised badly from the rocks and boulders she had hit as the water tumbled down. The water was freezing, and this too sapped her energy and strength. She looked around for something – anything – to grab hold of on the riverbank, but she was being carried along much too quickly and the bank was too far away. She struggled to swim a few strokes but it was as much as she could do to prevent herself being dragged under the water by the current. It seemed to be carrying her downstream very quickly – the river was running fast down towards the rapids. Kelly could hear a roaring noise in the distance as she was carried closer.

Her head slammed into another boulder, her face went under the water and she just found the strength to fight her way back to the surface. She coughed and swallowed more water. She thought she heard someone calling her name but it was hard to hear anything clearly with the rushing waters in her ears and the pounding of her blood in her brain.

She was feeling dizzy now, and faint, with the spinning, the pounding and the constant struggle to breathe. She was pulled under again, and in her panic reached out to try to grab onto something. Then her hand did touch something, and she grasped it. A hand was pulling her to the surface. Another arm grasped her around the waist, and pulled her out of the water.

She lay on the bank in the morning sunshine, coughing and gasping for breath. She felt sick and faint and dizzy. She closed her eyes to see if the dizziness would go. But someone kept shaking her and calling her name. She opened her eyes again and to her surprise saw her mother bending over her. She was back in Tim's bedroom. Sunlight streamed through the open window and below, from the kitchen, she could hear and smell bacon sizzling as Mrs Rabb cooked breakfast for them.

"Kelly! Come on – you'll be late for school," her mother was saying. And then, astonished, "But Kelly, you're soaking wet – you'll catch your death of a cold! How on earth did you get so wet?"

CHAPTER EIGHT

"I still don't believe it," said Stewart. "You weren't in the jungle. You were lying in your beds snoring your heads off. I heard you."

"Didn't you dream anything, Stewart?" Tim asked.

"Nah," said Stewart. "You and Kelly are making it all up as usual – I don't believe a word of it. I didn't see..."

He paused and frowned.

"Well...OK...I might have – maybe I *was* in the dream – on the edges of it, sort of thing. Yeah...I remember now. I saw the moon, and the stars. I was lying by the river and I could see the jungle...but that's all. I don't remember any more than that."

"I think it takes a few goes for it to work properly," Tim said. "The first couple of dreams I had, I only saw things vaguely, you know, like it really was a *dream*, but this time, well, it...I was really there. Just like Kelly said."

They were in the school playground at Monday lunchtime.

Now some of the other boys from the class ran up holding a football.

"Hey! Stewart," one of them called. "Want a quick game?"

Stewart nodded and turned to Tim and Kelly.

"See you later," he said and ran off.

"They never ask us to play," Tim said.

"No," said Kelly. "They don't. We're outsiders, Tim. I don't think they like us very much."

"Maybe they'll get used to us one day," said Tim. "At least Stewart's all right."

"Yeah," said Kelly. "Look Tim...what are we going to do? I mean, about the dreams? It's...it's getting too scary. When I was in the river...I thought I was going to die. I really did. If you hadn't pulled me out..."

"Lucky you drifted in close to the bank," said Tim. "I was able to reach you. It is odd though, that tiger could see you. Nobody else could."

"Yes, I've been thinking about that," said Kelly. "When I was walking down the path towards the camp, a squirrel ran away from me. It must have seen me as well. Tim... these dreams are getting more real each time. It's almost like *I'm there*. This time animals could see me. Next time, maybe people will be able to see me too."

"Yeah," said Tim thoughtfully, "it was more real for me this time. I suppose it depends a bit on the person trying the lantern. You went right into a dream, first time, whilst Stewart didn't; and I've needed a go or two before anything much happened. It probably depends on how many goes you have. The more times you use the lantern, the more real it is."

"Tim," said Kelly frowning. "Listen. I'm...not going again. It's too dangerous. Supposing someone sees me? Or...supposing I get stuck there? I might not be able to get back here again. Mum said it was really difficult to wake us this morning."

Tim giggled. "It's lucky she believed that story you told her about how you'd spilled a jug of water over yourself in the night! As for going back...yes, I suppose it is a bit risky. That tiger nearly got you, Kelly. The thing is... we were supposed to be trying to find the key for Aunt Irene's treasure chest. That's why we went. But we didn't come across any clues in the dream, so we're no further forward."

"Look, Tim," said Kelly. "The key might not be in the dream at all. It's probably lying around at home somewhere. We need to have a really good look and I bet we'll find it."

"OK," said Tim, "but there's another thing. Kelly...I'm worried about Aunt Irene. Those people I overheard in the dream, you know, the ones in the camp. They don't like her, Kelly. They don't like her at all."

Kelly stared at Tim in amazement. "What...what are you saying?"

"We need to protect her, Kelly."

"Look...she doesn't...*didn't* need protecting. *We know*

what happened. She came back here after her adventure and bought a house and lived here till she was an old woman. She *must've* been OK...if anyone needs help, it's the Prince!"

It was Tim's turn to stare. "But—"

"Yeah," said Kelly heavily. "I know. We know what happened to him, too. It's no good, Tim. We can't get involved any more. If...if we go back, and I'm more solid and they can see and hear me, *and* I somehow persuade the Prince not to make that silly climb, and he doesn't get killed, then, don't you see, Tim? *I won't be able to come back here!* This place – you and I and Scotland and Aunt Irene living in the house here – *it won't have happened!* Aunt Irene will probably end up living in India, we'll still be living in England and...who knows?"

Kelly was crying now, her shoulders heaving.

"That's why we can't go anymore, Tim! Don't you see?"

Tim stared at the playground.

"Yeah," he said quietly. "I see."

*

After school they cycled home through lowering clouds, not speaking much. Each of them was preoccupied with their own thoughts. It was late October, the day before Halloween and already almost dusk. Ahead of them up the hill, they could see Aunt Irene's house – their house – with lights shining out like a beacon in the half darkness.

The kitchen was warm and bright and they sat down hungrily. Mrs Rabb had prepared a shepherds pie which Tim and Kelly demolished before settling down to their homework. Tim grunted.

"Huh," he said. "You'd think Miss Moondancer would let us off homework the night before Halloween. I've got to get my costume ready."

Mrs Rabb, who was clearing the table, pricked up her ears.

"Och, aye, well you know what they say in the village, my darlings?"

Kelly sneezed.

"No, what? What about?"

Mrs Rabb paused, dishcloth in the air.

"About your teacher, my darlings – that Agnes Moondancer." She paused again, then leaned forward confidentially. "They say down the village that she's a witch!"

"Oh, that," said Tim scornfully. "We've heard about that, Mrs Rabb."

"I can see you don't believe me," said Mrs Rabb, with all the dignity she could muster. She leaned forward again. "That's because, stuck up here, you don't see what goes on at night. She goes a-walking, does Miss Moondancer. She goes out at dead of night, with her cat sometimes, and she don't come home till nearly dawn. She's dressed all in black she is, when she goes out - and she *never* says a word about it. Nary a word. Now," she said, wagging her finger at Tim and Kelly. "What d'you make of that then, eh?"

Kelly coughed.

"So what?" she said. "Just because you go for a walk in the middle of the night doesn't mean you're a witch!"

Mrs Rabb drew herself up to her full height, which was only just taller than Tim and Kelly.

"You've not lived long in these parts, Kelly McTavish, so maybe you don't understand. *No one* goes out for walks at night around here, see? If you do, you must have a reason, and what other reason could she have?"

"And there's another thing," she went on. "What about this Halloween parade, eh? Every year, she gets all the kids to dress up and parade past her, ghosts, witches, ghouls and what have you. It's on again tomorrow night, isn't it? Well, don't you think that's weird?"

"It sounds fun to me," said Tim.

"We're not Americans," said Mrs Rabb grimly. "We're Scots - we don't celebrate Halloween. There's only one reason why she gets you to do it. It's so she can see if any of the kids are suitable to learn the black arts – that's what it's for, mark my words. It's a sort of a...a spooky talent contest...so she can find some kids to teach her witchcraft to.

"Believe me," said Mrs Rabb. "She's a witch! No doubt about it. No doubt at all."

PART TWO

KIMBUSTAN, 1936
CHAPTER NINE

The view over the valley in the early evening was breath-taking. From the castle terrace, high up in the hills of Kimbustan, Irene could see for miles. Far away, glinting in the sun, she could see the river and beyond that the jungle where they had gone hunting. A little nearer, rising towards the castle, were ribbons of fields interspersed with the occasional dwelling or small hamlet. It was late October. The harvest was almost complete and the fields had a sort of brown, hazy, dusty look. Closer towards the castle, the ground, still far below, began rising steeply. A sheer rock face fell away from the wall of the terrace and, by leaning over the parapet, Irene could just see that the vertical drop to the ground below was all of two hundred feet or more.

The main entrance to the castle was behind her. A narrow valley to Irene's left contained a snaking path which wound steeply up to a drawbridge. The castle was old and very well defended. It had been built over a thousand years ago and had withstood many attacks over the years by hostile neighbours from the surrounding countries. It had withstood everybody, in fact, until the British came.

The British did not launch an attack on the castle. They didn't need to. For the Kingdom of Kimbustan, high in the foothills of the Himalayas, was landlocked. It did not have access to the sea and in order to trade with the rest of the world, goods had to be shipped out through surrounding countries. When Ruhal's grandfather found that the British had taken control of all the surrounding Kingdoms and therefore controlled his access to trade, he thought it wise to come to an agreement with them. Kimbustan came under British control ("Protection" the British called it) without a shot being fired.

The British were not anti-monarchy and, as a result, the Kimbustani royal family were able to retain their title, position, and wealth. In theory, they also continued to rule. Under British protection, however, the ruler was "advised" to consult the British on all new laws before they came into effect and of course the British found reasons to advise against any proposed laws they judged to be against their own interests. The presence of several thousand well-armed and well-trained British troops on Kimbustani soil ensured that it was an unwise monarch who did not invariably take the advice of his protectors.

The British were in favour of administration and order and Kimbustan undoubtedly benefited from the schools, hospitals, roads, railways and other improvements built with the aid of British capital, British expertise, and Kimbustani labour. Kimbustan's economy had done well under British rule and over the years the average Kimbustani had become used to the British presence. Yet beneath the surface there lurked a latent sense of hostility to their British overlords.

Irene knew something of this. Like an iceberg, however, the full extent of the people's hostile feelings were hidden from her. So when Baku, the Prince's manservant, appeared on the terrace with a tray of cold drinks, Irene took one and smiled at him as he bowed to her.

"Baku," she said. "Have you seen Prince Ruhal today?"

Baku bowed again. "The Prince is busy with the preparations for his initiation, Miss McTavish. However, I believe he will see you this evening at dinner."

Baku's face was expressionless, but an observant person might have noticed a faint glimmer in his eyes. He bowed again and withdrew.

Irene sighed and sipped her drink, alone on the terrace – a large balcony really – in the late afternoon sunshine. It seemed remarkably hot for the end of October – an Indian summer, they called it here. Charika had warned her that the weather at this time of year could change incredibly quickly. The warm summer breeze and hot sunshine could be replaced by winter cold and lashing rainstorms in a matter of hours. Irene, watching a dragonfly pass lazily by, found this hard to believe.

A sudden peal of laughter from indoors interrupted her reverie and a moment later Ashwina, Pari and Agnes burst onto the terrace, laughing and shouting. They had evidently been playing hide-and-seek and Agnes was rather red in the face from the exertion.

Irene had noticed a change in Agnes over the past few weeks. In Delhi and Bombay, when Irene had first arrived from Scotland, Agnes had been every inch the governess with her pupils. She had been tense and withdrawn, clearly weighed down by the pressures of her position, and Irene had been worried about her. Now she seemed much more at ease, even happy.

"Pari, you fool!" shouted Ashwina, happily. "It was wicked of you to hide in the battlements when you told us you would be in the basement!"

"All those stairs!" said Agnes, smiling. "Pari, Ashwina is right. You are a wicked girl for deceiving us!"

Pari sank down on to the seat beside Irene and regarded her governess. Her face was perfectly grave, but her eyes had a twinkle in them.

"Oh, Miss Moondancer, I am so sorry," she said. "What will my punishment be?"

"Bread and water for two weeks; and no stories before bedtime!" replied Agnes, and all four of them burst out laughing.

"Irene, please play with us," begged Ashwina.

But Irene shook her head.

"It's so peaceful here," she said. "I love this castle."

"That's just as well," said Agnes, suddenly serious. "You are likely to be spending the rest of your life here, eh, Irene."

Irene looked around at the solid turrets and battlements, at the snow-covered peaks behind and at the river vista in the distance. Despite the warmth of the afternoon, she shivered. She suddenly felt a very long way from home.

"I hope you girls won't be too tired this evening," she said, to change the subject. "Your father has promised us a special surprise after dinner. I wonder what it could possibly be?"

To Irene's own surprise, her question did not provoke a very enthusiastic response. Ashwina mumbled something about being tired whilst Pari simply stared into space.

Agnes clapped her hands together twice.

"Now girls," she said, "it is time for you to rest. It is a special occasion this evening, as Irene said. Tomorrow your father will be busy. Tomorrow night, he performs the tiger climb; and the next day is the wedding itself. Many guests will be coming including the British High Commissioner and a special Guard of Honour from the Cavalry Regiment. There will be all manner of festivities, of which tonight's small gathering is only the first. So girls, if you are tired, rest now. You will not have much time to rest tomorrow."

The girls looked at each other and then, slowly and reluctantly, they got up and trailed downstairs to rest.

Irene let out a sigh. "Oh, how I'll miss you Agnes, and the girls too," she said quietly.

"Och, you'll still see us - we'll be around most of the time," said Agnes.

But Irene once again shook her head.

"I know that, of course," she said. "But, don't you see, Agnes, once I'm married I'll be a Princess, won't I? And then I'll have to behave like one too. I won't be able to play hide-and-seek, or go out horse riding with you like we did this morning, or even share a joke or a laugh with you. People will be watching me. I'll be expected to behave like a member of the royal family. So, yes; I will miss you."

Agnes stared into space. For a while, neither of them said anything. Slowly the sun moved towards the far horizon.

Then Agnes looked directly at Irene and took a deep breath.

"Irene, you know we've been friends almost all our lives; since our first day at school together. Now I need to speak plainly and to tell you the truth."

Irene said nothing, but stared at Agnes' face which, uncharacteristically, seemed to reflect a state of inner turmoil.

"Irene, listen, I was – am – in love with His Royal Highness. I've been in love from the moment I saw him – well before you arrived, Irene. Of course, he's not in love with me. To tell the truth, I don't think he even notices me, really. Well, why should he, indeed? He has hundreds of women admire him every day, but...it does hurt so. I feel pain every time I see him – every time I'm in his presence. I..."

She paused, her face screwed up and then continued.

"I'm not jealous of you, Irene, you must believe that. I'm glad it's you getting married. I'm glad you're happy and in love. But the thing is this: I decided a long time ago, after that ball, that although my own heart sings whenever I see him, I wouldn't want to be his Princess. I couldn't live here, Irene. I just couldn't. I couldn't take the attention. I love the Prince, yes, for what that's worth. But don't you feel the eyes in this castle following you everywhere? Don't you hear the whispers behind your back? You're going to be on a pedestal, Irene, and I couldn't cope with that."

Irene was frowning now. She stared at Agnes.

"Agnes, I'm just an ordinary girl from Scotland. I don't plan to change who I am. Why should people put me on a pedestal?"

It was Agnes' turn to sigh.

"Irene, you just will be, that's all. You'll be a member of the Royal family and that's what happens, believe me. But Irene, dear, there's another thing – and I don't know how to say this. You must know, don't you Irene, that the Prince had...still has...other women?"

The colour drained from Irene's face.

"Agnes! How dare you! It's not true!"

Agnes' eyes dropped to the floor, her shoulders sagged, her hands twisting together.

"You need to know the truth, Irene. Ruhal is rich, charming, and handsome. Every woman in the kingdom wants him. Many of them try and some of them...succeed. You can't blame him, Irene, and I don't think he's in love with any of them. For what it's worth, I think he does truly love you. But you need to realise that, married to you or not, these other women will still exist for him."

She sighed again. When she looked up, there were te in her eyes.

"Irene...I'm sorry. I really am. I know you love him. I know how much this hurts, but I had to tell you...you do see that, don't you?

Irene sat perfectly still for a minute. Then her body heaved and the tears and sobs spilled out. After a while she stood, still crying, and tottered to the balustrade. The sun was on the far horizon now, a blood-red colour, its last rays falling weakly on the darkening scene below.

Agnes rose, and stepped to Irene's side. Still looking out towards the horizon, Irene spoke jerkily. "Agnes - I know - I still love him..." The tears flooded out again. "What...what on earth...am I to do?"

CHAPTER TEN

"I wish you were coming, Kelly."

Kelly sneezed.

"Yes" she said. "So do I, but Mum won't let me and that's that. Anyway, I do feel sort of woozy."

She sneezed again. "At least you'll be with Stewart, and you'll be back quite soon. I don't suppose it'll go on all evening."

Tim pulled the tiger skin around his shoulders.

"I'm sorry you've got flu. Probably falling into that river didn't help. Tuck yourself up in bed – I'll tell you all about it when I get back."

"Yeah," said Kelly thickly. "I think I'll go and lie down for a bit. Bye, Tim."

It was cold and dark outside as Tim fetched his bike and began to freewheel down the road towards the village. A stiff wind was blowing and low clouds scudded across the sky. Tim felt a few drops of rain on his face. It looks as if a storm is brewing, he thought. His tiger-skin costume wasn't very warm, and he shivered.

The lights of the schoolhouse were a welcome sight. Tim parked his bike and pushed his way inside. Forty or fifty school children, dressed up as ghosts, goblins, ghouls, vampires, werewolves, witches and other assorted horrors, flocked around the hall. There was no sign of his teacher. Tim pushed his way through the throng and found Stewart, dressed as a goblin and talking to Conall.

Conall looked daggers at Tim as he arrived. He grunted and moved off.

"Hi Tim. Where's Kelly?"

"Got flu. Where's Miss Moondancer?"

"Oh, she don't come here," said Stewart. "She waits on the bridge."

"What bridge?"

"You know, the one over the stream near the beach. This is what happens, see? We all parade out of here, down the high street, across the bridge and round back here. Miss Moondancer waits on the bridge and we march past her. Then she follows along. When we get back here she gives a prize for the best costume, and then we all go out again, trick-or-treating in the village. Finally, we have some hot cocoa and biscuits and go home."

"Sounds quite OK to me," said Tim.

"Yeah," said Stewart. "It's just a waste of time, that's all."

At that moment, a small, slight woman with large spectacles – Miss Bird, the assistant schoolmistress

— climbed up on the stage, clapped her hands, and in a small quavering voice, called for silence.

"Now children, it is time for the parade. Off we go!"

The children obediently lined up in a crocodile and stepped out of the schoolhouse door.

*

"It's really blowing up out there," said Mum as she and Dad sat snugly in the living room, a blazing fire in the hearth.

Dad grunted. He had his feet up, his slippers on and was reading the paper.

"I hope Kelly's all right," Mum went on. "She's tucked up in bed, but I think she's got a temperature. Do you think we should get the doctor?"

Dad grunted again.

"Are you listening?" demanded Mum. "What was I saying?"

Dad looked up hastily.

"Oh, er... yes dear, erm...yes. I'm sure she'll be fine."

Another gust of wind hit the house and the electric lights flickered. Mum glanced out of the window.

"I feel sorry for Tim, out in this storm." she said.

"Oh, he'll be back soon," said Dad. "As far as I can tell this parade's only a bit of silly fun. A bit of weather never did anyone any harm."

"Yes, well, I suppose that's true..." said Mum.

And she went back to her knitting.

The wind seemed to have strengthened significantly, even in the brief time they'd been in the schoolhouse, thought Tim, and the rain had started now too – a heavy downpour had begun. Wet and bedraggled, the children started down the village street towards the beach, their high spirits rapidly dwindling as the storm hit them.

"Argh, this is awful!" muttered Stewart, as a gust of wind and rain caught him full in the face.

A few of the smaller children began to cry. Miss Bird, the only adult amongst them, called out in a shrill voice.

"Children! The weather is just too bad for the parade this year. Turn around. Back to the schoolhouse please!"

The children turned to go back, but Tim stood his ground.

"I'm not going back," he called. "Miss Moondancer will be waiting!"

"Och, lad, she'll be inside, snuggled up with a good book in this weather," said Miss Bird. She had to raise her voice to make herself heard above the wind.

"I'm going on," said Tim stubbornly. "You take the others back, Miss Bird."

Another gust of rain and wind caught them as they spoke. Miss Bird began to quickly shepherd the children back up the street.

"Be careful, Tim McTavish," she said over her shoulder. "It's a wild night tonight, that's for sure..."

Tim stood and watched as the group hurried away from

him. Why had he said what he'd said? He didn't know. Then one boy – Stewart – broke away from the group and trotted back to him. Tim grinned.

"C'mon, Tim," said Stewart. "Let's go see that old witch!"

*

The wind whistled around them as they made their way down the main street. Beyond them, they could see the sea, angry now and with great waves washing onto the beach below. The moon came out briefly but was soon hidden again behind great swathes of dark cloud.

The village council had found the money to install street lighting some years previously and the harsh sodium glare cast sharp, deep shadows. Debris from the storm whirled around them: leaves, sweet wrappers, old cereal packets. Another burst of rain hit.

"This is barmy," shouted Stewart above the wind and rain. "Why are we doing this?"

Before Tim could reply a large and violent gust of wind shook the houses around them; and all the village lights went out.

"Power cut," shouted Stewart. "It happens sometimes, especially if there's a storm. Don't worry, it's usually fixed by morning."

It was harder to see in the darkness, but just then a flash of lightning lit the sky and Tim saw with relief that they were almost at the bottom of the village street, near to the corner leading to the bridge.

Mum carried a candle into the living room and placed it on the mantelpiece.

"Any luck?" she said to Dad.

He shook his head. "It's not the fuses," he said. "I reckon the power's out in the whole village. We'll just have to wait till it's fixed."

"At least we've got a warm fire," said Mum, "and enough candles for a while. Ah well, the pleasures of living in the highlands!"

She smiled. "You know, I'm settled in this house now - I like it here. I didn't think I would, when we left England, but...it's so peaceful."

A crash of thunder interrupted her and Dad laughed.

"Not very peaceful at the moment," he said. "How's Kelly, by the way?"

"She was fast asleep when I looked in on her," said Mum. "You know, it's very dark up there. I think I'll light that old lantern of Tim's and put it in her room, just in case she wakes."

"Good idea," said Dad. "That should keep her out of harm's way."

CHAPTER ELEVEN

Kelly tossed and turned in her sleep. She felt hot and cold in turns, her head hurt and her throat was sore. She woke for a moment. It seemed very dark, and she could hear a storm outside. Her sheets were wet with sweat. She rolled over and went back to sleep...

She could hear the shutters banging as the wind caught them. From down below came, faintly, a sort of rhythmic chanting sound. That's funny, Mum and Dad must be playing records. Haven't heard that one before though...

A vivid flash of lightning outside, followed by a cavernous crack of thunder. The rain lashed down and the shutters banged. Another brilliant flash; even though her eyes were closed, the covers pulled over her ears, it was hard to keep the storm out. Something seemed wrong somehow. It must be the flu, Kelly thought – I don't feel right at all.

The shutters banged again and Kelly slowly opened her eyes. It was pitch dark, but Kelly knew now that something was really wrong. She didn't have shutters on her bedroom window.

The chanting below rose in pitch. Kelly strained her eyes in the darkness. She seemed to be lying on some sort of rough bed, with cushions, quilts, and blankets thrown onto it higgledy-piggledy. A flash of lightning outside provided sudden illumination and Kelly saw that she was lying on a couch in the corner of a large, high-ceilinged room. An old mirrored wardrobe was against one wall. There was a large double bed against another wall, and ...

It went dark again. Kelly caught her breath. Where was she? She had a sneaking suspicion that she was back in India, although how could she be? Maybe it was a dream, after all. She still felt very woozy and hot.

Another flash of lightening outside, and the chanting downstairs stopped. Simultaneously, through the wall from the room next door, a piercing scream rang out, and Kelly suddenly felt very cold and shivery indeed.

*

Tim battled along the seafront, the wind tearing at his costume, Stewart at his side. To his left waves washed onto the rocks. The beach was a little further on after the bridge. On the right, the dark hills of Scotland rose high into the clouds, their tops invisible in the rolling mists. The air was full of rain and spray, wind and thunder.

Up ahead he could just make out a tall, dark figure silhouetted against the sky. Shivering, Tim pulled the tiger skin tighter around his shoulders and put his head down against the wind, quickening his pace toward the bridge.

*

A figure sat up in the double bed opposite, and struck a match. Kelly instinctively froze, the blankets pulled up over her, peeping out between the cushions. A candle flared into life and Kelly caught her breath. It was Ashwina.

"Pari! Wake up!"

Ashwina was shaking someone, who was apparently sleeping next to her in bed. Pari gradually sat up and rubbed her eyes.

"Ashwina? What's...what is wrong, Ashwina?"

"Didn't you hear it Pari? That scream?"

"Ashwina, you dreamt it...let me sleep..."

"Listen!"

The two girls sat up in bed, listening. Then Kelly heard it. The chanting had stopped, but from below there rose a hubbub, cries, shouts and then wailing.

Ashwina and Pari did not speak. Both somehow knew that something terrible had happened and they shrunk down onto the bed, close together. Pari's body shook with silent sobs. Ashwina put her arm around her, her own face tight, screwed up against tears.

Kelly longed to jump out of her hiding place, run over to them and comfort them; but at that moment the door of the bedroom was thrown open and Queen Shikari strode in.

107

Irene was hysterical, Charika could see that. These British, she thought, outwardly so calm but underneath they are like children. Not like an Indian – outwardly excitable and voluble, but inside, in the soul, there is calmness and peace.

The other one though – Agnes Moondancer – Charika had to admire her. She kept her head in a crisis, no doubt about that. Now she was bending over Irene, who was crouched in a corner, her eyes wild, her hands covering her face, speaking soft, soothing words to her.

"Irene...come now, come now. Don't distress yourself...it may not be as you fear..."

"Agnes! He's dead, Agnes! I know he is!" wept Irene. "Oh...Ruhal! Ruhal...don't leave me..."

Irene wrapped her arms around herself tightly and began to rock her body from side to side.

"Oh...Ruhal! He's dead! Oh, what am I to do...?"

"Irene...listen. Whatever's happened, has happened, and I'm afraid that there is nothing that you or I can do about it. We'll just have to try to make the best of things. Now, compose yourself, my dear, and let's try to think what to do..."

"I want to die..." moaned Irene. "Oh, Ruhal..."

"Now listen to me – both of you," said Charika, going over to them. "The Prince is dead. You must leave here at once!"

Irene stopped crying and stared at her.

"Leave here...why?"

"Listen," said Charika grimly. "Listen hard."

From the courtyard below came a confusion of sounds - shouts, cries and wails - but now also an angry murmuring, an undercurrent of sound that made the blood run cold.

"I told you before," said Charika. "Miss McTavish, they blame *you* for our Prince's death. My people have... hatred...real hatred...in their hearts. You are foreigners and I – I cannot protect you. Indeed, I am afraid for you. Please, you *must* be quick; there is no time to be lost!"

At these words Irene gave a sort of gasp and clutched the amulet around her neck. Slowly she stood up.

"Come, Irene," said Agnes gently. "Let's go and pack."

As if sleepwalking, Irene allowed herself to be led to the door, Agnes holding her arm. She stood for a moment, her eyes suddenly swivelling around, as if taking in everything for the first time: the room, Charika, Agnes, the window, and through it the turret, dome, and flagpole opposite.

"I'll never forget this scene," she said, almost whispering. "I'll see it in my mind's eye for ever..."

Agnes caught her wrist. "We both will," she said softly. "We'll always remember tonight – always."

"And – and the Prince?" asked Irene, desperately.

"And the Prince," said Agnes firmly. "Twenty-five, fifty, a hundred years from now, we'll always remember Prince Ruhal – I know we will."

"Yes..." breathed Irene.

And together they went to gather their possessions.

Chapter Twelve

Her scream hung in the air, in the darkness, drowning out the sounds of the storm. Tim was stunned. He didn't know what he'd expected of Miss Moondancer when he got to the bridge – didn't know or understand what this strange Halloween parade was really about – but he'd never expected this reaction. The image of her seemed to be burned into his brain: a bright flash of lightning, followed by the look of absolute horror on her face, dissolving to sheer animal terror as she caught sight of him for the first time.

Tim could see nothing now. He and Stewart stood waiting for the next flash of lightning.

And then he saw her, on the beach, on the firm sand by the seashore. She was running, hard, away from them.

"Miss Moondancer!" Tim yelled. As the lightning fizzled, he jumped the parapet of the bridge, as she had and hit the ground running, chasing after his teacher.

Kelly kept perfectly still, peeping out under the blankets and listening to the Queen talking to her granddaughters. In an abrupt but very matter-of-fact tone of voice she told them what Kelly had already guessed: that their father was dead – killed in the fall from the top of the turret.

Kelly had to marvel at the composure shown by both girls. They seemed to accept his death with equanimity. Indeed they hardly said a word. Kelly realised with a jolt that these children, young as they were, had already known much grief and sorrow in their lives. They had already lost their mother. Now their father was dead too and they were orphans.

A noise at the entrance to the room caused Queen Shikari to turn abruptly. Agnes and Irene stood in the doorway, momentarily rooted to the spot.

Agnes immediately curtseyed to the queen, who returned the obeisance with a nod. Irene seemed too shocked to notice her surroundings fully. Although her eyes were now dry, her face had a glazed, vacant look as if she were somewhere else entirely.

"Your highness," said Agnes, by way of explanation. "Miss McTavish is naturally very distressed at present - please forgive her."

The Queen inclined her head again.

"And so, what are your plans now, Miss Moondancer?" she asked.

Agnes looked momentarily surprised by the question.

"I ask," the Queen said, "because I feel that, in view of the delicate situation in the Kingdom presently, and bearing in mind the somewhat controversial nature of my son's betrothal—"

"Your highness," said Agnes firmly. "Miss McTavish and I will be leaving as soon as possible. That's what you want, isn't it?"

There was a shocked silence. Then, for the first time since Kelly had encountered her, the Queen smiled.

"Miss Moondancer, I see that we understand each other very well," she said. "To be frank, I fear for your safety. My people blame you for my son's death. I think it would be as well for you to leave as soon as practicable. Indeed I suggest you depart by first light."

"Your highness, we are already on our way to pack," replied Agnes. But as she spoke, she caught sight of Ashwina and Pari, huddled together on the bed, and looking more crushed by that statement than by the news of the death of their father. Neither Ashwina nor Pari made a sound, but Agnes ran to them and threw her arms around them both.

"Girls, please do not be sad," she said. "Listen: Irene McTavish needs me now. I must look after her. You have Charika here and she loves you as much as – more than – I do. And there's Jaideep too – he'll need his older sisters more than ever now. Please, oh please, don't cry – you'll only make this the harder for me, that you will."

Ashwina and Pari clung tight to her, Pari with her face buried in Agnes' skirt, Ashwina sitting proud and stiff as a statue. The tears they had been holding back welled out at last and it was all Kelly could do, hidden under the blankets, to keep her own eyes dry.

Then she saw Agnes bend to Ashwina's ear and whisper something. The look on Ashwina's face changed. It softened and she saw Ashwina bend in turn to Pari and repeat the whisper.

Queen Shikari had been standing with her back to them, looking out of the window to the courtyard below and totally ignoring the scene on the bed. Now she turned.

"I shall go and speak to my people," she said. "Perhaps I can calm them, take the sting from their hostility. I shall return."

With that, she swept to the doorway past Irene, who was still standing there, dazed and motionless, and disappeared down the corridor.

"Come, Irene," said Agnes with a sigh. "Let us go and pack – all four of us. The girls are coming too."

*

As soon as they had gone, Kelly emerged cautiously from the bed and crept to the middle of the room. The storm was abating now, but the odd flash of lightning still lingered in the lowering sky.

She stood in front of the old wardrobe mirror and looked hard at her reflection.

"Nothing!" she whispered under her breath. She could see no trace of herself in the mirror: she was still invisible. "Thank goodness for that!"

A flash of lightning lit the sky, and in it, Kelly could just see a white, shimmering, translucent outline of herself. The flash faded and as it died, so too did her reflection. In normal candlelight it was unnoticeable.

"I've got away with it - this time," she muttered. And then she made for the door. Clearly many things were happening tonight in the castle and Kelly wanted to make sure she knew exactly what was going on.

*

Who would have thought a seventy-year-old woman could run so fast? thought Tim. He was running flat out along the hard sand at the edge of the sea, Stewart behind him, yet it was all he could do to keep his teacher in sight.

The rain had lessened a bit now and the moon had come out. They ran across the sand, wind in their hair, jumping the waves and puddles. Black outcrops of rock loomed near – some half submerged into the sea, some running up through the soft sand towards the cliffs.

Tim gathered his breath.

"Miss Moondancer – wait!" he called, but his words were grabbed by the wind and hurled away. His teacher gave no sign of having heard, her pace quick and even across the sand. The beach stretched for miles at this point, all the way from the village to the headland. Tim had no idea why they were running, why indeed his teacher had been so terrified, but he knew, deep down, that he must keep Miss Moondancer in sight. He was gasping now, out of breath, a stitch starting in his right side. He forced himself to keep going.

"Tim!"

It was Stewart, gasping. "Tim...I can't...I have to stop..."

Tim raised his hand in acknowledgement and ran on, without looking back. They had covered a couple of miles at least by now, he thought. Stewart would have to catch them up later. Tim was focused, totally, on holding his pace, trying to keep up with Miss Moondancer. As he ran, he found himself thinking back to his time at school in England – or more precisely to his time after school, to his training sessions with the cross-country team. They had trained almost every day in the late afternoons, in the cold, wet, dark weeks between late October and the end of March. Tim, in his mind's eye, could see and hear his coach, yelling and shouting, encouraging him to hold on, hold the pace to the finish line, even though his chest was heaving, his lungs were bursting, and his legs felt like lead weights. His team had won quite a lot of races that way. Tim smiled to himself and almost unconsciously he stood up straighter, pumped his arms hard, and lengthened his stride a little. Maybe – just maybe – he could win this race too.

It seemed to Tim for a while, as if the laws of time and space were suspended. He could still see his teacher a hundred yards ahead. The moonlight streamed down on them, and in it his teacher seemed to shimmer, her feet dancing and floating effortlessly over the sand. The beach was wide at this point and the flashes from the storm made it difficult to see clearly. Tim had no idea whether he was gaining on

Miss Moondancer, or she on him. He forced himself to keep going.

The rain returned, and with it the clouds. In a second, the moon went out and Tim was running through darkness and water, brilliant flashes and cracks of thunder. He was wet to the skin. This is dangerous, he thought, out here in the storm, on my own, wet through – if I'm struck by lightning, who would know, and who'd be surprised?

Tim couldn't see a thing now. It was pitch black. He forced himself to slow down. I can't risk running into a rock, he thought. As he slowed, the wind fell for a moment and suddenly, very clearly, Tim heard a cry of pain from just ahead. The wind rose again and another squall of rain hit in the pitch blackness. He edged forward, gingerly. Suddenly the cloud lifted, and Tim saw his teacher, half sitting, half lying on the sand, clutching her leg. She had obviously put her foot in one of the depressions in the sand caused by the outgoing tide, fallen, and twisted her ankle.

As Tim approached, she looked up, fearfully, like a wounded animal caught in a trap; but then her expression changed to a look of relief.

"Tim! Tim McTavish! Is that you?"

"Miss Moondancer! Are you hurt?"

"I...I fell, Tim. I..."

"Are you OK, Miss Moondancer? Can you stand?"

Miss Moondancer tried to rise to her feet but as she put weight onto her ankle, her face distorted with pain and she cried out involuntarily. She collapsed to a sitting position again.

"It's...it's no good, Tim. It's my ankle...it twisted as I fell. Let me...let me rest a little...whoa!" She smiled. "That was quite a run, back there, wasn't it?"

"Yes," said Tim simply, watching his teacher. At the back of his mind he was wondering what to do, what was going on and what was going to happen next.

"I haven't run that fast in years," said Miss Moondancer. "Good to know my old legs have still got some life in them. Now, let me try again..."

She started to struggle to her feet once more. Tim darted forward anxiously.

"Wait! Miss Moondancer..."

"Hey! Hallo there, Tim." It was Stewart, puffing, red faced and out of breath. "Phew! I'm wet through! Oh! Miss Moondancer? What's happened? What's going on?"

Tim quickly explained that Miss Moondancer had fallen, and needed help. Stewart frowned.

"Look, the first thing to do is to move her out of the wind, and try and get a bit of shelter from the rain. Then one of us can go for help."

It was good, clear thinking and Tim was grateful for that. The moon was shining brightly again now and Stewart spotted an overhang of rock, low down under the cliffs, about twenty yards away.

"Miss Moondancer," said Stewart. "If you can get to your feet, Tim and I will support you, one each side. Then maybe you can hop on your good leg, and Tim 'n' me will help you down."

A few minutes later, Miss Moondancer was newly ensconced in a more sheltered location. Her ankle was swelling badly now and it was clear that she had no hope of walking on it.

Stewart looked at Tim.

"Right," he said. "I'm off to the village. I'll get my dad out and help will be along in no time. Tim, you stay here and keep Miss Moondancer company."

"Yes, OK," said Tim. He smiled wanly.

They both watched as Stewart began jogging slowly back along the beach to the village.

And then Miss Moondancer began to speak.

*

Agnes threw open a bag and began stuffing clothes in it. They were in Irene's bedroom. The children had been sent back to their own room to gather their possessions.

Irene watched listlessly.

"What are you doing?" she asked.

Agnes looked up. "Irene, you know we have to leave," she said patiently. "I'm trying to pack some of your clothes for you. We can send for the others later."

"Oh..." said Irene, uncomprehendingly.

She still seemed to be daydreaming. She's in shock, Agnes thought. She left the packing and went over to her.

"Look," she said more gently. "I'm sorry, Irene, really I am. I know how hard this is for you, but please try to understand. We need to leave here, and quickly. Now, pull yourself together and give me a hand with the packing, there's a dear."

That seemed to get through to Irene and she straightened up, and even managed a smile. Her eye fell on the packing, and then she suddenly gave one of her little gasps, her hand clutching at the amulet around her neck.

"Agnes, my dowry, the treasure. We must take it with us! Ruhal – he gave it to *me*. We can't leave it here. It's *mine* now, and it's going with us..."

She ran to the end of her bed, grabbed open the treasure chest and began transferring the jewels into the open jewel box.

*

The young princesses were throwing their own things into a bag in their room. Theirs was a frenzied sort of activity; stupor had been replaced by action. Charika watched them silently, saying nothing, but her eyes followed their every move.

Pari held up a particularly ugly sari.

"Should we take this?" she asked. "I hate it, only Daddy gave it to me for my birthday..." Her voice trailed off. She suddenly stopped and stared at Ashwina.

"Ashwina, what are we doing?" she asked. "How – how can we think of leaving? We are Princesses, Ashwina — of royal blood. Who is to continue as monarch if we leave? What is to become of our Kingdom? And what of Jaideep? How can we possibly leave him to grandmother? I..."

She stopped, put her head in her hands and sobbed.

"You are right, Pari," said Ashwina, after a pause. "We cannot leave. But keep packing. I've an idea..."

*

Kelly followed the twisting passageways inside the castle. So many rooms! And all filled with heavy furniture, dark brooding portraits, deep exquisite rugs and drapes.

She came to a staircase and followed it down. There seemed to be no one about inside the castle. She guessed that everyone was in and around the courtyard she had glimpsed from the bedroom window.

The staircase led to a large hallway, which in turn opened into a long passage. Kelly tried one door at random, and found herself in a scullery. This led through to the kitchens, also deserted. and then to a pantry followed by a small hallway, and finally after going through yet another short passageway and more steps, Kelly found herself outside in the courtyard itself.

The courtyard was a large one, enclosed on all sides by the walls of the castle. A large number of people were there, gathered at the far end around a woman standing on a raised platform. The rain had mostly stopped, although it was still windy, and the moon was bright. There was an occasional roll of thunder in the distance but the storm seemed to be passing.

Kelly walked towards the crowd. As she approached, she realised that she knew the woman on the dais – it was Queen

Shikari herself. The crowd was listening quietly but even so Kelly couldn't hear what the queen was saying. She pushed around the outside of the crowd, towards the front.

"The British stole our Kingdom," Queen Shikari was saying. "They rule over us. We must obey *their* laws, not ours. They have no respect for our ways, our customs, our religion..."

This doesn't sound right, thought Kelly. I thought the Queen came down here to quieten the crowd...

"And now *they* are responsible for the death of *your* Prince. Oh yes, do not be deceived, my people. The British caused the death of my son. Have they not sent a Harlot to turn his head? Have they not sent a Witch to cast a spell of deceit and illusion over Ruhal and his daughters? These women," – the Queen paused, and then went on – "these dogs, these she-wolves, they plotted the death of my beloved son..."

Someone in the front – Baku, the Prince's servant – shouted out: "Kill them! Let's kill them now!"

There was a murmur from the crowd.

Someone else called out:

"Baku, *no!* I don't believe it. How could *they* have done this? The Prince fell – we all saw him. It was an accident, it must've been,wasn't it?"

There was another murmur. The Queen held up her hand for silence.

"Listen to me. You want proof? I tell you, even now, those devils are planning and scheming. They plan to rob us – rob us blind. They have already stolen Ruhal's life, oh yes, but now they plan to steal the crown jewels themselves, and they expect to sneak out of here at daybreak, like rats..."

The crowd was murmuring again, but Kelly was not listening. She was already halfway across the courtyard, running for the pantry door, as fast as her legs could carry her.

Chapter Thirteen

"You, you scared me, Tim, that's why I ran," Miss Moondancer said. "In that costume, dressed in a tiger skin, I..."

She paused, then continued.

"You know, it's fifty years ago tonight since Ruhal's death..."

She took a deep breath. Tim glanced at her. Her fists were clenched tight as if she were gripping hard onto something.

"I still see him, in my dreams, sometimes. Up on that roof, in his tiger skin, reaching for the flag...or dressed in his finery, like he was the previous evening. We'd had a beautiful dinner, then...afterwards...he said he had something very special, something for Irene..." she stopped again suddenly.

Tim was watching her now, discreetly, his lids lowered.

Her hands had relaxed but her face was screwed up, her eyes shut tightly. She took another deep breath.

"I loved him, Tim. There, I've said it. You know, in fifty years, I've never told another soul. Well, except Irene, of course, but I don't know if she was listening. It was hard to get through to her sometimes. Yes, I loved him...but so did a thousand others. Irene was the one who caught him..."

She stopped again and sniffed. Her eyes had opened and she was looking at Tim.

"Well, there's no point in going on about it now," she said, a little of her old spirit returning. She took yet another deep breath. "It was a long time ago and best forgotten. What good does remembering do, eh?"

Tim could not think of a reply and for a while they both sat silently, their backs to the rock, looking out to the sea. The storm had not abated. Indeed, it seemed to have gathered in strength and both were grateful for the shelter provided by the rocky overhang.

The wild night was beautiful in its own way. Sometimes the full moon shone brightly, casting its pale light over sand and sea. Black rocks, hard shadows, wind, spray, foaming waves and scudding clouds. Sometimes, when the moon was obscured by heavy cloud, it was pitch black, punctuated by brilliant flashes and flickers of lightning and cracks and rolls of thunder, like some heavenly fireworks display. They felt and heard the howl of wind and the rain squalls lashing the beach and sea in front of them. During these periods they could hear, but not see, the raging waves; indeed, could not even see each other, such was the totality of the darkness about them. Who would have believed that the forces of nature could be so powerful? Tim thought. It was as if the heavens themselves grieved and wept and raged and railed against the untimely death of Ruhal, Prince of Kimbustan.

*

"Irene, what are you doing? What are you thinking of?"

Agnes spoke in the tone of voice she normally reserved for ticking off naughty children.

Irene straightened up, a diamond brooch in her hand.

"I told you, Agnes. This is mine now. Ruhal gave it to me. I'm not leaving without it."

"Irene, listen – listen carefully. This treasure, these jewels, you can't take them, Irene. The treasure has to stay here. It's not yours."

"Not...mine? But Ruhal... it was my dowry, Agnes! Of course it's mine!"

Agnes spoke slowly and patiently. "Irene, please listen to me. This treasure was not Ruhal's to give. It's state property – it's their crown jewels. Any king or queen, prince or princess, has the right to wear these items, but they don't belong to them. Ruhal...well, he liked grand gestures. I know he probably told you it was yours. He always liked to impress, but you'll have to leave it, Irene – all of it."

Irene was staring at Agnes now, a look of rage on her face.

"You're ...you're lying, Agnes Moondancer! Just like you lied the other day about Ruhal...about his girlfriends. You

127

would have done *anything* to stop me marrying him, and now you'll do anything to stop me...remembering him..."

A loud murmuring from the courtyard below interrupted her.

"Don't you *see*, Agnes? This," – she waved her hands around the treasure – "this is all I have of him now. I don't even have a picture..."

She bent, her shoulders heaving helplessly, and again began to transfer the treasure to her bag.

"Irene, I'm not going to argue with you," said Agnes desperately. She did not like the sounds from the courtyard below. They seemed to be getting louder and more urgent, and she privately thought they should leave even before daybreak, but she was not ready to leave the subject of the treasure completely.

"That amulet, Irene...yes, even that amulet was not Ruhal's to give. Why do you think the girls were so upset when we talked on the terrace yesterday? That amulet belonged to Ashwina's mother. She left it to Ashwina when she died. Ruhal had no right to take it from her. And that ridiculous story he told us about it after dinner! And giving it to you as something very special, in front of everybody, in front of Ashwina..."

Irene was staring at her, wide-eyed. She seemed speechless.

An angry murmur, lower and more insistent than before, rose from the courtyard. Agnes checked herself.

"Come on! I think we'd better get going right now. Let's go and get the girls."

She turned for the door, grabbing a bag. Irene picked up her own bag and the jewel box and followed obediently.

*

Tim wondered what he was doing here, in a tiger skin, sitting on the beach, watching the storm. It all seemed so...inevitable...as if it had all been planned by somebody, somewhere. The storm made his head spin. Once again, time and space seemed suspended. He had no idea how long they had been sitting waiting for rescue.

To take his mind off all this he turned to his teacher.

"Miss Moondancer, why do you do it? The Halloween project, I mean," he added. "I just don't understand – what's the point of dressing up and having a parade and so on?"

Miss Moondancer sniffed, in her spinsterish schoolmarm way.

"I do it because the kids enjoy it," she said. "There isn't a lot for them – you – to do around here, Tim, you know. We're a long way from the nearest town and we need to make our own amusements."

"But, why make us write about it?"

"Creative writing. It's just a teaching exercise. Why," asked Miss Moondancer, her voice a little strained, "are you asking about it, Tim McTavish? Don't you want to do the homework I give you?"

"Oh, no, Miss Moondancer – it's not that. It's...some of the kids think, well, some of them...say you're a witch," Tim finished in a rush.

129

Tim thought his teacher would be angry or shocked. Instead, he heard her sigh in the darkness beside him. Then she said quietly, "I know Tim. People have always said that about me, even when I was in India. What I've done to deserve that reputation, I don't know." She laughed hollowly. "I tell you, Tim, if I could say a magic spell right now to get us home to our safe warm beds, instead of sitting here in the rain and cold with a broken ankle, well, d'you think I'd hesitate? Take no notice of the other kids, Tim – it's what *you* believe that's important, isn't it?"

"Yes," said Tim. "I suppose so."

Miss Moondancer sat quietly for a minute. Then she said, "Let me ask you a question, Tim. Do you believe in ghosts?"

Tim stared at Miss Moondancer, or rather, would have done if it weren't so dark.

"Ghosts?"

"I saw one once," said Miss Moondancer. "It was a long time ago, Tim. It – it saved my life..."

Tim did not get the chance to reply to this surprising statement, for a voice shouted from the darkness just then: "Tim! Miss Moondancer!"

"Phew," said Tim, relieved. "Rescue at last. This must be Stewart and his dad. Stewart," he shouted, "over here!"

It was Stewart, but it wasn't rescue. He was alone.

"Tim! The tide's coming in. I can't get back to the village – we're cut off. We're in trouble, Tim. In an hour's time, this whole beach will be under six feet of water!"

CHAPTER FOURTEEN

Kelly was panicking, her heart beating fast as she tried to find her way back to the bedrooms. *If only I'd paid more attention as I left Ashwina's room,* she said to herself despairingly. *I must get back, I simply must; I have to warn Aunt Irene.*

The corridors in the castle were endless, each with numerous doors, all closed. There seemed to be a number of staircases. *I can't even remember what floor I want,* she thought. She ran from room to room, corridor to corridor, floor to floor until she didn't even know how to make her way back to the kitchens again.

From time to time, loud angry sounds erupted from below. Sometimes Kelly could hear shouting, sometimes just a menacing babble. Once or twice she heard loud sharp cries. These caused Kelly to quicken her pace. But no matter how many doors she tried, how many corridors she ventured along, none of the rooms contained Irene, Agnes, Ashwina or Pari. Indeed, the castle seemed deserted. Perhaps Irene and Agnes have already gone, she thought. Perhaps they too heard the commotion and have already left, quickly, quietly and discreetly.

Anyway, she thought to herself, why am I trying to find them? I *know* they got home safely.

But what about Ashwina and Pari, said a small voice in her head. You don't know what happened to them...

Another voice - the voice of reason - started to speak. You can't, *mustn't* change anything, it said. You may change the future and then you won't exist.

Shut up, said Kelly savagely to that voice.

Another roar arose from below and she ran on, down some stairs, along a corridor, up more stairs, around a corner. It's like a bad dream, she thought, like a nightmare...and then she remembered – it was a dream, sort of...wasn't it?

She stopped, uncertain now of anything, feeling lost, alone and bewildered – and then she saw them. They were emerging from a room near the end of the corridor, Agnes carrying a bag and walking rapidly in the opposite direction from her, followed closely by Irene, who had a bag in one hand, and – Kelly gasped – the old jewel box in the other.

Almost crying with relief, she hurried after them, as they turned the corner into Ashwina's room.

*

"There's only one thing to do," Miss Moondancer said.

Her voice was quite teacher-like now, as if they were back in the village school and she were giving a lesson.

"Tim, you and Stewart should try to climb to safety. I'll stay here."

Tim stared at his teacher in dismay.

"Miss Moondancer, we're not leaving you," Stewart said. He had a determined look on his face.

"Stewart, you will do as you're told," Miss Moondancer said crisply. "I've broken my ankle. I cannot climb. You can. Now, please, do not argue."

"Miss Moondancer, if we leave you here, you'll drown!" said Stewart desperately.

Miss Moondancer opened her mouth to reply, but at that moment Tim said,

"Hold on. I....I've just realised where we are."

It was Miss Moondancer's turn to stare at Tim.

"I believe we are on the beach, Tim McTavish. Now is not the time to be flippant, young man."

"Miss Moondancer, we're just below our – Aunt Irene's – house. And there's a path down to the beach from there. It must come out around here somewhere!"

"But, so what?" asked Stewart. "Miss Moondancer's got a broken ankle. She couldn't climb any sort of path."

"No...but we could, and then we can get help – adult help – and they could come down with us and carry Miss Moondancer up the path!"

Tim had a triumphant look in his eyes.

"Yeah, OK," conceded Stewart. "But you're going up alone, Tim. I'm staying with Miss Moondancer. You'll find your way to the house quicker than me, once you get to the top, and your parents can summon help by phone. But, come on, let's be quick. The tide's coming in fast."

*

Ashwina and Pari were dressed and packed when Agnes and Irene hurried in. Charika was still standing in a corner of the room, watching and listening silently.

The noises from the courtyard were becoming particularly unpleasant now. The crowd seemed to be whipping itself up into a frenzy. It's lucky Irene and Agnes don't understand the local dialect, thought Pari, for several slogans – "Hang the Harpies!" "Burn the witches!" and "Revenge for Ruhal!" were some of the milder – were being repeated in a chant by the rabble below.

"Come on, girls, let's get going," said Agnes.

Charika stepped forward.

"It is too dangerous for you to leave by the main entrance," she said. "The crowds are everywhere. They want revenge and you cannot face them."

Agnes said, "Is there a back entrance we can use?"

Charika smiled. "There is an even better way for you to escape. You can use the secret passage."

"Secret passage?"

"All castles have secret passages for events such as these," Charika said. "Rulers generally need to be able to leave in a hurry, and without detection. That's why these passages were built."

Ashwina clapped her hands.

"Of course! You're right, Charika," she said. "Come on, Pari, give me a hand."

To Agnes', Irene's, and Kelly's great astonishment, Charika, Ashwina and Pari went to the side of the old mirrored bedroom wardrobe and pushed hard. The wardrobe slid away to reveal a roughly-hewn passageway with a steep, narrow flight of steps leading down into the darkness below.

"We'll need a candle," said Ashwina, taking one from her bedside. "Charika will stay here and push the wardrobe back into place when we've gone."

Kelly was watching from the doorway. Whilst the others had been intent on the secret passage, Kelly noticed that Irene still seemed strangely detached. She saw a vacant stare on Irene's face, punctuated occasionally by the odd flicker of emotion. Irene frowned and fumbled in her pocket. She produced a carved sandalwood box. She opened it, checked the contents, closed it, then replaced it in her pocket. Most of the time, though, she simply stared out of the window at the rooftop and the flagpole opposite.

So, when Agnes said, "Come on Irene, let's get going," Kelly was not at all surprised to see Irene turn around to Agnes with a blank look on her face.

"Go...?" she echoed. "Go, where?"

Agnes, normally cool under pressure, was running short of patience.

"Irene, you are in shock," she said. "And that's caused you to suffer loss of memory. Now listen to me. We need to leave this castle *now*." Agnes spoke slowly and deliberately, as if to a small child. "We've already discussed it and we've both packed our bags – see..."

She pointed to Irene's bags. "So, Irene, it's time to go now – come on!"

"I'm not going," said Irene. "I...don't want to."

"Come on!" said Agnes again, more forcefully. "It's not *safe* to stay, Irene – really it's not!"

As if on cue, there came a bloodcurdling roar from the courtyard below.

Kelly knew she had to do something fast, and damn the consequences. The rabble was screaming now and she knew that their lives were in danger, but she suddenly realised, with a shock, that there was little or nothing she could do. The others couldn't see or hear her. Up to then Kelly had thought this an advantage, but now she felt powerless to help them.

"I'm not leaving," said Irene in a matter-of-fact way.

But then the emotion returned, and she spoke jerkily.

"I...***Ruhal is here***, Agnes. He's not even been buried yet. I can't leave him. I can't!"

She sat down on the bed and put her face in her hands.

The others looked at each other.

At that moment, two things happened at once. One was another, tremendously loud roar from the courtyard, followed by the thunderous sound of shouting and running feet from directly below them, in the corridors of the castle itself. The second was that Kelly had her big idea.

*

Tim and Stewart stood at the bottom of the path gazing up towards the house. Miss Moondancer sat on a rock nearby.

The path had turned out to be only a few yards away from where they were sitting. The moon had come out for a while and the storm seemed to be easing slightly. Nonetheless, Tim had a sinking feeling in his stomach as he stared up at the long climb above him. Don't use the path, his father had said, it's too dangerous. Nah, Stewart had said one day, let's go back by road, the rock's too crumbly...

"C'mon," said Stewart. "You need to get moving, Tim. The tide'll be in before we know it."

Tim glanced round at the sea. The waves were certainly a lot closer. He took a deep breath.

"OK," he said. "Wish me luck. I'm going up."

*

Charika stepped through the door and along the passageway.

"I'll see if I can head them off," she called. "I'll tell them you're in the other wing of the castle."

Agnes turned to Irene.

"Irene, you can't be with Ruhal now," she said. Her voice was sympathetic but tinged with desperation. "We simply must get going. Come on, girls."

Ashwina and Pari were already standing by the entrance to the secret passageway, both holding candles.

Irene looked up, straight at Agnes.

"You go, if you want. I'm staying. I was Ruhal's fiancée... his wife almost. My place is here...Oh!...Oh my God!"

Irene's eyes, slowly widening in fear, were now fixed on the doorway. There was a look of terror on her face. Involuntarily, she clutched at the amulet around her neck.

Agnes looked around to where Irene was staring. Ashwina and Pari grabbed at each other in fright.

Standing in the doorway, in the very spot where Kelly had been, was a ghost. Not that anyone in the room could see its face, or its features, but it was a ghost all right. It had to be...

It was an odd thing though, almost a caricature of a ghost. It looked for all the world like a white sheet floating in mid-air, its ends trailing a foot or more above the floor, arms flapping as it glided slowly towards them.

Irene was standing now, each person in the room inadvertently backing away from the ghost in the door-way, towards the secret exit. Pari gave a little scream of terror.

"Oh...Oh my God!" said Irene again. And then, as one, they turned and ran into the secret passage, almost leaping down the rough-hewn steps and into the hidden world beneath the castle.

Kelly slipped off the white sheet she'd picked up in Irene's room. Her ghost idea had worked superbly. She smiled to herself and followed the others into the secret passage.

A moment later, Charika returned. She gave a sigh of

relief to find the room empty. Then she rolled the wardrobe back into place.

She had sent the rabble to search the wrong part of the castle but she knew it would only be a matter of time before they realised the deceit.

CHAPTER FIFTEEN

The passage dipped and twisted as it descended into the depths below the castle. Kelly was grateful for the candles held by Pari and Ashwina. Agnes and Irene, in the confusion, had not brought one. They hurried along through the dark, gloomy passages.

The panic was gone now, now it was clear that the ghost – or whatever it was – was not following them. They remained nervous, however, and when the shadows thrown by the candles flickered and wavered on the rough walls, Ashwina and Pari were inclined to jump and clutch each other for safety.

Agnes ignored the shadows, but listened out nervously in case her ears provided reason to suppose that the rabble – or the ghost – were pursuing them. The acoustics were not good, and the echoes thrown off by their own feet caused her to stop frequently and listen for evidence that the entrance to the secret passage had been found.

Irene appeared oblivious to her surroundings, still clutching the jewel box tight to her.

Kelly, of course, remained the unseen member of the group. She followed along as best she could, but Ashwina and Pari, who were leading, set a cracking pace and it was all Kelly could do to keep up with them.

The passageway seemed to go on for miles. There were relatively few straight sections. The tunnel builders, in an effort perhaps to find the softer rock, had incorporated a large variety of disorienting devices – bends, steps, ramps, low ceilings, twists, turns and narrowings. After a short while none of them had any idea in which direction they were heading. Fortunately, there seemed to be only one route to follow so they kept going.

They came at length to a much wider portion of tunnel, with a greatly increased ceiling height. The air seemed fresher here and Kelly guessed that they were in some kind of natural cave, hopefully not too far from the exit.

Suddenly, Ashwina gave a cry.

"Oh, look. We can't go on. The way forward is blocked!"

It was true. At the far end of the cave a rock fall had blocked the way forward. Large, heavy lumps of rock had fallen from the ceiling. It would be impossible to shift them.

Irene stared at the rocks for a minute and then gave a little sigh. She found a boulder in the middle of the cave and sat down on it, her shoulders drooping. Yet in despair, something indefinable seemed to have changed again within her. Kelly, looking at her, couldn't tell why she thought this; but something about her face, her whole demeanour, made it seem that perhaps the old Irene was back again.

Ashwina walked over and sat down by her, followed a little later by Pari. Agnes remained standing, staring at the pile of rocks.

They sat quietly for a moment and then Irene turned to Ashwina and Pari.

"I – I'm sorry, girls...I think we'll have to go back, back to the castle. We can't get through this way."

*

The wind was whipping at Tim's clothing as he climbed, the night black as pitch. At least the rain's holding off, he thought.

The first part of the climb hadn't been too hard. Steps were set into the rock, narrow and steep but firm underfoot. The path had zigzagged across the face of the cliff. Tim, climbing higher, had looked down once, during a lightning flash. He had glimpsed the pale upturned faces of Miss Moondancer and Stewart, far below, the lightning flickering on them. Miss Moondancer had her eyes shut. Her arms were stretched out towards him, her forefinger pointing at him. Her lips were moving, as if she were praying. Tim had felt vertigo. He had immediately thought about how high he was, how he mustn't fall...

Tim had looked straight ahead at the steps in front of him. He didn't look down again.

Now the steps gave out. Tim found himself on the proper path, a narrow sloping ramp traversing the face of the cliff. Can't be far to go now, he thought. Can't be far to go...

*

They sat quietly on the boulder for a moment, the three of them: Irene, Ashwina and Pari. Irene took their hands in hers.

"I'm sorry," she whispered. "We must go back to the castle, girls. There is no other choice."

Ashwina squeezed Irene's hand and smiled shyly at her.

"Pari and I always planned to go back." she said. "We can't leave Jaideep – we can't abandon him to Queen Shikari's clutches, but we thought that if we didn't come with you at least this far, to the end of the secret passage, you wouldn't leave the castle in the first place."

Irene stared at her for a moment and then her face crumpled.

"Oh, Ashwina...oh, Pari..I've been a fool, haven't I? I've been a danger to us all. I...we...could have left earlier...I... could've not married him. I shouldn't have said I'd marry him – then none of this would have happened, would it? Oh, what a fool I've been! Ashwina, please forgive me, and Pari, you too. I've taken your father away from you...it's... it's *all my fault*!"

The words came tumbling out higgledy-piggledy, followed by tears. Pari gently stroked the back of Irene's hand.

"Irene, what happened was an accident. It is fate, Irene. Karma, as we say. It was destined to happen and nothing we can do can change what is destined. What will be, will be. So, please, do not blame yourself."

For a moment, it was as if Irene had not heard, but then she stopped crying, lifted her head and smiled at Pari. Slowly, she reached behind her neck and undid the clasp of the amulet she was wearing.

"I...I think this is yours," she said softly and handed the amulet to Ashwina. "When you wear it, Ashwina, remember Ruhal. Remember your mother and father, won't you? Wear it wisely, my child, and guard it with your life..."

"Now," she said in a louder voice, "I think we'd better get going, hadn't we? We don't want to be late back for breakfast!"

It was a very bad joke, considering what awaited them back at the castle, but Pari and Ashwina both giggled out loud. Kelly smiled too and glanced across to Agnes, who was still standing by the rock fall. She stood, feet slightly apart, facing the rocks. As Kelly watched, Agnes slowly raised her arms, her forefinger pointing forward at the rocks. Her eyes were closed, and she was muttering something hard under her breath, over and over again.

And then it was as if a miracle happened, for as Irene and the girls stood up, the ground quivered slightly. There was a loud rumbling, and then more rocks began to fall from the wall near the far end of the cave – small ones at first, then larger boulders. Dust filled the air; the girls began to cough.

Then Pari shouted, "Look, daylight!"

*

They wandered out, four girls and a ghost, through the newly formed opening in the side of the cave, into the early morning sunlight. The storm had quite gone, blown away in the night. In its place was a beautiful morning: a blue sky, and a warm, soft breeze. Other than a certain dampness to the ground, there was no evidence that the storm had ever happened.

They emerged at the bottom of the rock face below the castle veranda, where they had all sat one afternoon two or three days ago. To Irene it now seemed like months or years before. In front of her was the same vista she had gazed at from the balcony. The path to and from the main entrance of the castle led down the hill to their left.

Irene gazed at the scene in front of her, till Agnes gently tugged her sleeve.

"Come Irene. It's time we were away."

"Yes," Irene breathed. "Oh, yes..."

Then she turned to Ashwina and Pari.

"It's been a strange time, hasn't it? You know, I hardly feel as if any of this is real... It's like a strange dream and I'll suddenly wake up and won't be here on an Indian hillside, fleeing for my life. Maybe I'll be back in Scotland, I don't know..."

She looked at Ashwina and Pari. "Is this real, or am I dreaming? Tell me girls, and did we really see a ghost back there?"

"I think a lot has happened to us in a very short space

of time," said Ashwina. "But that's the way it is, some-times. I don't think this is a dream, Irene. My father really is dead...and...I think you are in danger. I don't know about the ghost. We certainly saw something, but maybe it was just a shadow. We didn't stay long enough to find out, did we?"

"That earthquake just now was a bit strange, though," said Pari. "This isn't an earthquake area – we never have quakes – but one came along at just the right time, didn't it?"

"Yes," said Irene. There was a pause. "Maybe someone up there is looking out for us."

"Stuff and nonsense, Irene," said Agnes briskly. "If some-one up there were looking out for us, we wouldn't be in this pickle in the first place. And Pari, you are quite wrong, you know. There must be quakes here regularly, otherwise the original exit wouldn't have been blocked, would it?"

She sniffed disparagingly. "Now girls, it's time for you to get back. Irene and I really must get going."

Irene looked at the girls.

"Oh, Ashwina, oh, Pari, how I shall miss you..." she said.

And then, once more overcome with emotion, they hugged and embraced till Ashwina pulled away.

"Miss Moondancer is right: you must go," she said. "Goodbye – we must get back before the Queen misses us."

Ashwina's face was tight but her countenance betrayed no emotion as she grasped Pari's hand and led her briskly back into the entrance of the cave. They stepped inside, without looking back, and then, as if a magic wand had been waved, they were gone.

"Agnes, do you think they'll be all right?"

"They are Indians, dear, and have royal blood. I'm sure the rabble will not harm them."

"I – I wasn't thinking of the rabble, Agnes. I was thinking of the Queen."

Agnes stared up at the castle above them. From this angle it had a dark, brooding look.

"Karma. We'll just have to trust to luck, dear. Those girls are no longer my responsibility, I'm afraid – but you are. Now, let's get going."

Irene turned for a last look at the castle before they set off. Together, they stared up at the dark turrets towering above them.

"Agnes, I – I didn't mean what I said, back there, last night - about how you'd do anything to keep me away from Ruhal. I know now that I was wrong. I'm...so sorry, Agnes...so sorry!"

Agnes embraced and hugged her. When they parted, Agnes sniffed a little; her nose was red and her cheeks were wet. And if Kelly hadn't known her teacher well, she would have imagined that she'd been crying as freely as Irene.

CHAPTER SIXTEEN

Baku shouted to the others: "Have you found them? Where are they?"

"They are not in the castle, Baku," yelled Tarun above the din of the rabble. "They must've given us the slip."

"Bah!" said Baku. He turned angrily to Charika who stood, stone-faced and with her arms folded, in the doorway of the girls' room.

"Where are they, woman? Tell me!"

"You are making a fool of yourself, Baku. I've no idea where they are and if I had, I wouldn't tell you. What harm have they done you, these two British girls?"

Baku went red in the face from anger. He brandished his sword at Charika.

"I tell you, woman, when we find them, the Jezebels, we will cut them to pieces!" he yelled. "They shall die for their deceit!"

He turned back to Tarun.

"Post lookouts on the castle veranda," he said. "If they've slipped out we shall see them on the road below. On horseback, it will be an easy matter to catch them."

*

The rain was lashing down again, making the rock slippery underfoot. Tim could hardly see a thing. Sometimes bright white flashes of lightning dazzled him, but mostly it was pitch dark. He was moving along by touch, high on a narrow ledge cut into the cliff. He was wet through, soaked to the skin and shivering with cold.

Tim had glanced up a while ago at the cliff above him. The wall seemed to rise sheerly up, the top swathed in mist and cloud. In the gloomy half-light, the rocks took on strange forms – turrets, domes, battlements bulged from the mist. He strained his eyes, trying to pierce the mist above him, trying to make out the top.

The lightning flickered and the cliff face faded into blackness again. Tim gritted his teeth and kept going.

He had no idea how long he'd been climbing. It was as if time was standing still. He was in his own little world now, a world consisting of wind, water, rock, great height and darkness. He was getting disoriented: why was he climbing and where was he climbing? He dimly remembered: Miss Moondancer was watching and the others too, in the courtyard below, but where was the flag? He had to get the flag, had to...oh, it's so dark, so cold...must keep going... keep going up...watch the rock, it's crumbly...Irene's waiting, waiting for me...she wants me to keep going...can't be far now, can't be far...

Tim reached some iron rungs, set into the face of the rock and began to inch his way up them.

*

Kelly was starting to feel woozy again. Must be the flu, she thought – it's coming back. She was following Irene and Agnes down the path, away from the castle, towards the valley. It was about seven in the morning now, she judged. The birds were singing and the sun was just rising above the mountains.

She happened to glance down at the path as she walked, and then caught her breath sharply. By her side was a faint but distinctive shadow – her shadow. I'm starting to materialise, she thought in sudden panic. Soon people will be able to see and hear me, and maybe I'll be stuck here for ever!

She pushed the thought to the back of her mind. I've got to see this through, she thought – I've got to. Some sixth sense within her told Kelly that the danger for Agnes and Irene was not over yet...not by a long way.

Agnes and Irene were talking as they walked down the road in front of Kelly.

"What do you think we should do now, Agnes?" asked Irene. "We've left the castle – now what?"

"We'll have to try to get back to Bombay," said Agnes. "From there, we can decide what to do next. We can take a

151

train from the town near here. Luckily, I have some money saved up."

Irene smiled. "You're so practical, Agnes. I don't know what I'd do without you, really I don't. Oh, Agnes, it's such a glorious day, and here we are, just the two of us, walking in the sunshine down this mountain back to freedom. I've – I've been such a fool, Agnes, haven't I? I know now that I would never have been happy, married to Ruhal and living in that castle. Oh, if only I'd seen that earlier, as you did, none of this would have happened."

"Well, love is blind, as they say," said Agnes. "These things are sometimes difficult to see because they are painful to take in. Still, let's put all that behind us now. Irene, you'll need to start thinking, dear. Do you want to stay on in India or go home to Scotland?"

"I think I want to go home, Agnes," said Irene. "I've had enough adventures to last me quite a while and I'm ready for a quiet life. I'd like to go home to Scotland and buy a big old house in the hills somewhere, overlooking the sea. That's my dream, Agnes, and sometimes when I'm there, I'll stand on the cliffs overlooking the ocean, in the moonlight, and remember Ruhal, and I'll be sad. But sometimes the sun will shine and children will play and gulls will wheel overhead, and then I'll remember the laughter we had, the good times, the friendships... Oh Agnes, my life's just beginning again, isn't it?"

Agnes said nothing, but she squeezed Irene's hand and smiled at her. They walked in silence for a while.

"Agnes," said Irene, "if...if anything should happen to

me, I'd like you to have this. " She lifted the jewel box she was carrying.

"Oh, Irene," laughed Agnes. "Nothing's going to happen to you – I think we've got clean away, dear."

But she spoke too soon. A cry rang out from the walls of the castle above them; and the chase was on.

*

Stewart stared up at the cliff face. It was hard to see anything. The rain had returned and with it the thunder and lightning. The centre of the storm seemed to be almost directly overhead now. Stewart had to wait for each flash of lightning to see how Tim was doing.

Beside him, Miss Moondancer's face was upturned. Her eyes were almost closed, her arm outstretched towards the cliff and she muttered constantly under her breath.

*

Baku, on horseback, pulled his sword from its sheath and held it aloft.

"My brethren, our mission is a holy one. We ride down now to avenge our Prince. Death to the she-goats! Death to the Harlots! Death to the foreigners!"

The gates of the castle were opened and the rabble poured out.

*

Kelly ran hard down the hill. On the road in front of her, where her shadow should have been, she saw, not a shadow exactly, but definitely a sort of outline. It seemed to be getting clearer by the minute. I am solidifying, she thought with a start - I'm becoming more real. And it's happening just when I want to leave.

In front of her, Agnes and Irene ran, Agnes leading. Kelly glanced over her shoulder. There was no sign of their pursuers as yet, but they all knew it was only a matter of time. The road bent around the slopes of the mountain and they could not see far along it, either ahead or behind them.

Kelly was getting a stitch in her side and the flu made her breath wheezy. She forced herself to keep going.

*

Tim could hardly see a thing. His eyes were dazzled from the lightning, his ears deafened from the thunder. He grimly hung on to the iron rungs, his tiger costume awkward and heavy about him. He had to go up, didn't he? Or was it down? No, it was up. That's right. Have to rescue Miss Moondancer, have to get the flag, it's at the top of the flagpole...

He took another step up, the wind whipping at him, his hands feeling above for the next rung. Have to keep going, keep going up...

*

They could hear the hooves thundering on the road now, behind them as they ran. Agnes, still leading, looked from side to side ahead of them, her eyes searching desperately for a hiding place.

There was none. They were on a bare stretch of mountain with no trees, boulders, not even a ditch to hide in.

"Agnes! I...I can't..."

"Irene! Drop the jewel box! You'll run faster!"

Irene, gasping for breath, clung tight to the box.

"No! I..."

"Drop the box, Irene!"

Agnes slowed momentarily and grasped Irene's arm. Together, they ran on, Irene still gripping the box tightly in her free hand.

*

Baku, riding a white horse, rounded the curve in the road and yelled in triumph.

"There! There they are!"

Baku had watched the British cavalry, training in the plains, had seen them on their chargers, galloping and slashing with their sabres. Now, in an unconscious parody of their action, he held the reins in his left hand and brandished his sword in the air with his right. He turned to Tarun riding beside him.

"You see! They run like dogs! And like dogs, they will be slain!"

"Baku," implored Tarun, "they are only women...only girls. Why kill them?"

"Bah! You are a woman, yourself, Tarun. We must avenge!"

Digging in his spurs, Baku pointed his sword and charged.

*

Almost there! Just a few more rungs to the top...and then...

*

"You know, it's almost midnight," said Mum. "I think we'd better turn in."

"Tim's not back," said Dad. "I'm a bit worried, I must say."

"It's such bad weather and with this power cut, I'm sure he's staying overnight with that boy Stewart," Mum said. "His mother is one of the nicer ones in the village – she's more welcoming than some of the others. She said she'd be happy to have Tim and Kelly to stay, any time. Yes, I'm sure that's where Tim is. Anyway, it'd be a dark, cold, and wet ride back up here on his bike, that's for certain."

"You're right," said Dad, relieved. "OK, let's go to bed."

Mum blew out the candle in the sitting room. As she did so, the grandfather clock in the hall began to strike twelve. Dong...dong...dong...

"Better blow out Kelly's lantern, too. We don't want a fire, do we?"

*

Kelly was running as hard as she possibly could. The others were still ahead, running for their lives. Kelly's stitch was hurting and she was very out of breath. Just as she felt she absolutely had to slow down to catch her breath, she heard a bloodcurdling yell from behind her. Glancing over her shoulder she saw Baku, his raised sword glinting in the sun, begin his charge. He was about five hundred yards behind, but riding rapidly towards the three of them. Behind him, the other horsemen from the castle galloped in pursuit.

Kelly's mind was working fast. She knew that Agnes and Irene still couldn't see or hear her. Nor for that matter could Baku, but perhaps his horse could see, or at least sense her. If she could get in front of the animal and startle it...

She began to sprint. As she did so, from somewhere a long, long way away but also, somehow, strangely inside her head, she heard the sound of a bell striking - like a clock chiming: ONE......TWO...... THREE...

*

The storm was reaching its climax.

The rain lashed down on the figure in the tiger skin, climbing the iron rungs. The air seemed full of sparks; the sky crackled with electricity. Sometimes, when lightning flashed, it was as light as day. Sometimes it was pitch dark, as though he were wearing a blindfold. The wind grabbed at him, but he clung on. He knew he had to keep going, going up. They were watching. He could feel their eyes on him from below, from across the void. He had a mission to fulfil.

A bell began to chime in the distance somewhere.

He gritted his teeth.

"Come on," he said to himself. "Let's count the chimes - make it easier..."

"ONE..."

He hauled himself up.

*

Who would have imagined that her friend could run so fast, thought Irene, as they sprinted down the road, Agnes still gripping her arm. She had tried to pull away, to stand and face the rabble, to give Agnes a chance to escape, but her friend had hung on grimly and forced her to run. Irene could hardly keep up, her legs flying down the hill. We can't outrun them, she thought in despair. We can't possibly get away – it's only a matter of seconds before they cut us down...

She realised that for some reason she had been counting under her breath.

"FIVE...SIX...SEVEN..."

Then she cried out in disbelief. On the road ahead were men in uniforms, British uniforms...

*

Captain James Fortescue, of His Majesty's Indian expeditionary force and on temporary attachment to the British High Commissioner for Kimbustan, was not best pleased when the Commissioner, having received an invitation to the royal wedding, ordered him to take a detachment of soldiers and march up to the royal palace, so as to provide an impressive British presence at the wedding ceremony.

"Just make sure you arrive a day early," his superior had said. "You are to provide the guard of honour. It wouldn't do to arrive after the festivities are all over."

Captain Fortescue thought the whole affair to be ridiculous. He didn't approve of mixed-race marriages, and there was enough gossip about for him to know that this one was bound to cause all sorts of trouble. Besides, he had met Irene McTavish, and had that dratted Prince not come on the scene, he quite fancied his chances with her himself. Not that she would make a suitable wife, he told himself hastily. The girl's family were, by all accounts, of very modest social standing and as a career officer in His Majesty's Armed Forces, he needed to make the best of whatever advantages may come his way. A wife of the right standing and social connections was a very definite asset. Nonetheless, he had a certain regard for Miss McTavish and did not like to see her waste her affections on, in his frank and not-so-humble opinion, that complete and utter bounder, Prince Ruhal.

James Fortescue had many faults, but he could think and act quickly when he needed to.

Now, sizing up the situation rapidly, he said, "This looks nasty. Fire a warning volley above their heads, Sergeant. Quick, now, look sharp. No time to lose."

"Aye aye, sir!"

*

"EIGHT...NINE...TEN..."

A crack of thunder, very loud, overhead...a bolt of lightning sizzled past.

He reached for the next rung...only one or two more...

*

As the shots rang out over his head, Baku, the cavalry man, discovered too late the difference between his own horse and one trained by the British. His horse, startled by the sudden volley, bolted down the path, straight towards the girls and the guns ahead.

Baku screamed, this time in terror, one hand pulling desperately on the reins, trying to pull his horse up and stop the headlong charge towards the British. He rolled helplessly in the saddle, his feet out of the stirrups now, his sword arm flailing wildly as he tried to keep his balance...

*

"TEN...ELEVEN..."

My lungs are bursting, thought Irene. Oh God, oh God, he's almost on us, and he's about to...

*

I'm almost there! Only chance...got to throw myself in front of the horse...

*

"Bring him down, Sergeant!"

As the order snapped out, Sergeant Williams, reputedly the best shot in the regiment, stepped forward, knelt, squinted down the barrel of his rifle, and pulled the trigger.

*

One rung to go...He could feel Irene watching him...

"TWELVE..."

As if on cue, the lightning flashed down, there was a bang of thunder, and the rock crumbled. The iron rung came away in his hand. He fell backwards. A voice screamed his name, as he'd half known it would.

Then everything went black.

*

It wasn't the sergeant's fault - he thought he had a clear shot. How was he to know that the bullet he'd fired at Baku had hit a ghost in the chest on the way to its target?

Kelly felt a searing pain in her ribs.

"Tim!" she screamed. "Oh, Tim..."

She felt dizzy. Everything was blurry, fading...then black.

*

The other horsemen turned and galloped back up the path, leaving Baku lying and bleeding in the dust.

Others of the rabble, who had followed on foot, turned and ran. Unnoticed, a shadow in the air flickered and floated above them.

Agnes and Irene staggered a few more steps and then collapsed at the feet of Captain Fortescue, panting and heaving. Irene's face was bright red, and her lungs felt fit to burst. Nevertheless, she felt oddly exhilarated at that moment - elated to be alive.

Captain Fortescue bent over them.

"Well, well, well! Misses McTavish and Moondancer, I do believe. And to what do I owe the pleasure of your company?"

"Captain Fortescue," gasped Irene. "The Indians believe that the British have no place, here in India. Until today, I agreed with them, but today, sir, today the British army saved my life. I am eternally grateful to you."

And with that, she fainted clean away.

Captain Fortescue looked up, to where a soldier was bending over the body of Baku.

"How is he, Corporal?" he called.

The soldier straightened up and turned to the captain, a stunned expression on his face. Young and inexperienced, it was the first time he had seen a shot fired in anger. "Sir," he said in awe, "he's dead, sir – shot right through the heart."

*

Ashwina and Pari stood by the Queen, watching the scene from the castle veranda. The girl's faces were expressionless. The only outward sign of emotion was to be found in their hands, gripping the balustrade tightly.

After the shots rang out, each of them saw a sort of shadow, a kind of ripple in the air, floating upwards from the scene of the shooting; floating upwards in the clear blue sky towards the sun.

None of them spoke.

PART THREE

Chapter Seventeen

Mrs Rabb shut her garden gate and, humming to herself as she usually did in the early mornings, began the long walk up to the hill from the village towards the McTavish household.

At least the electric power's back on, she told herself - that's a mercy, for sure. The house'll no doubt be in its usual mess – it's astonishing how much untidiness those two children can create in one day. And I suppose they'll be wanting their breakfast – that family can certainly eat, I'll give them that. Och, well, the storm seems to have blown itself out last night. It certainly was a big one, we don't get many like that, that's for sure. And it's a beautiful sunny day, so maybe the kids'll run off and play in the garden somewhere and let me get on with the housekeeping in peace...

Mrs Rabb sighed. Looking after the McTavishes was certainly a lot more work than looking after Miss Irene, even in the early days, when...

She thought back to those days, when Irene McTavish, fresh from her travels in India, had bought the house on the cliffs above the village. Mrs Rabb had been a girl then herself, and still at school, just a few years younger than Miss Irene. At first Mrs Rabb's mother had kept house for Miss Irene and Mrs Rabb had helped out after school, but later, when she'd left school, Mrs Rabb had taken over.

Those days were happy ones, although she had to admit that Miss Irene could get a bit pensive sometimes, especially around this time of year. Miss Irene had never liked Halloween – she'd usually go to bed early with a good book, or so she'd tell Mrs Rabb the next day. But most of the time Miss Irene had seemed happy enough. She hadn't talked much about India but Mrs Rabb had heard one or two stories over the years.

Mrs Rabb hadn't said anything when, a few months after Miss Irene had settled in, a large portrait of an Indian gentleman – a Prince – had arrived from India, and was given pride of place in the hallway. A tiger-skin rug had accompanied the portrait. Miss Irene had sighed as she unrolled this, and had placed it with care on the polished wooden floor of the hallway. She'd looked down in the mouth, or even downright tearful, but she'd gone for a long walk along the cliff tops that afternoon with Miss Moondancer and had appeared at teatime that day with rosy cheeks and much more cheerful than she'd been when she'd gone out. She had never mentioned the portrait, or the rug, again and Mrs Rabb had judged it better not to ask too many questions, although she had a shrewd idea as to who the gentleman in the portrait was.

At first, when Miss Irene was young and pretty, Mrs Rabb had expected her to marry. Certainly there was no shortage of gentlemen callers. Mrs Rabb remembered one in particular, a Captain James Fortescue, who had apparently been out in India with Miss Irene. But Miss Irene didn't seem much interested in romance, and after a while he'd faded away and married some society girl from Edinburgh instead. That was before the war, of course, and by the time the war was over, and young men were available again, Miss Irene had settled into contented spinsterhood.

Yes, Miss Irene had seemed happy enough most of the time – going for long walks with her great friend Agnes Moondancer and helping the women's institute do their charitable work around the village. She and Miss Moondancer had even joined a running club and gone jogging for a time. She apparently had done some running of some sort out in India. Mrs Rabb frowned. She disapproved of young ladies undertaking masculine activities, as she thought them, and she was glad when Miss Irene stopped her jogging after a few months. Not Agnes Moondancer though. She had gone on to win quite a few local and county championships, had that one.

There had certainly been a bit of a commotion in the village last night, Mrs Rabb thought to herself disapprovingly. All those children coming back after their night of carousing around during Halloween, she supposed. Not that she'd seen any of it – she'd stayed in bed. Mrs Rabb frowned. It had been very late, well after midnight, she thought, but there'd been a great deal of noise outside her cottage. The noise of the storm, of course, but also running and shouting. Once even a loud bang like a gun or a rocket or something. Those children letting off fireworks, she supposed. Terrible, what their parents let them get up to nowadays.

Well, it really is a glorious day, she said to herself, as she went up the path to the McTavish household. It was warm and the sun was shining brightly. It's as if the storm last night had never happened, never happened at all.

CHAPTER EIGHTEEN

Kelly moved through the inky blackness. She was very cold and her chest hurt terribly. She could hardly breathe. Was she dead? I didn't think being dead would hurt this much, she thought. She was very tired too, could hardly move her arms and legs – it was like swimming through jelly or treacle.

She could see a light up ahead, a long, long way off. She struggled towards it. Then, behind her, she heard the sounds of hard breathing, of something chasing her. She looked around. Baku was there, on his horse, his eyes wild, his sword flailing, riding after her, but as Kelly looked, he and the horse began to shrink, to change into a growling, panting, black and yellow creature: the tiger. It was chasing her, its large eyes never blinking as it gathered itself to spring... But it didn't spring at her. Instead, it gathered speed and pulled alongside her, turning its head towards her as it did so. The tiger had a flag in its mouth, fluttering in the breeze as it galloped past. It winked at her and Kelly realised that the tiger wasn't a tiger at all, but Tim. He was running hard, chasing something. She tried to call out, to ask him to help her, but he ran on, ran past her, towards the light...

She was alone again, swimming in treacle, struggling along a long, long tunnel of darkness towards the light ahead. Then the light faded, and was gone. She slipped back into oblivion.

She could see the light again, bigger and brighter now, a round shining orb. Near it was a dark orb, frizzy and indistinct. She swam towards the light.

Everything was hazy. She tried to reach out for the luminous ball but her arms were covered in treacle and weighed down with lead. Then the dark orb spoke.

"Hello, Kelly."

She managed to force open her eyes. She was lying in her bed at home. The bright orb was the sun, shining through her bedroom window. The dark frizzy object was Tim, sitting on the end of her bed. His face was bruised and his head was heavily bandaged. He reached out and took her hand.

He was gazing at her bedside table. Kelly turned her head, and saw the lantern, its charred wick protruding from the neck of the lamp.

"Kelly, are you all right?"

Kelly nodded, coughed and grimaced with pain.

"What about you, Tim? What's happened to your head?"

Tim grinned at her. "I'll be fine. The doctor says it's just bad bruising."

He told her what had happened the previous night, leaving nothing out, up until the time he fell.

"Stewart's the hero of the hour, though. He'd seen me struggling near the top of the cliffs and had already begun to climb to help me. When I fell, I apparently landed on a ledge near the top. I must have banged my head then. Stewart says I was unconscious. Anyway, he managed to complete the climb, got up here and got Mum and Dad to raise the alarm.

"Luckily, the phones were still working, despite the storm and the power cut. Dad phoned down to the village and got them to launch the lifeboat to rescue Miss Moondancer. They sent the maroon up, and got the lifeboat launched OK. It managed to get around to our beach just in time to take Miss Moondancer off, before the tide reached her.

"Another group, the mountain rescue team, came up here. Stewart showed them where I was. They managed to abseil down the cliff to me. I was just coming round, apparently. They got a harness on me and were able to winch me up to the top of the cliff.

"Anyway, we didn't get to bed till a couple of hours ago. Miss Moondancer was brought up to the house here, at Mum's insistence. There's no one to look after her at her house and she can only just hobble along, so she's sleeping on the couch downstairs. Stewart stayed up here as well – he slept in my room. The doctor came up to look at my head and Miss Moondancer's ankle. He's coming again this morning."

"All in all, it was quite an adventure, Kelly. There is

one thing that's odd, though." Tim frowned. "When I was climbing the cliff, I don't remember seeing that ledge, the one I fell to. In fact, I'm sure it wasn't there, but when I fell, it just...appeared."

Before Kelly could answer, there were footsteps on the stairs and the door opened. Stewart entered carrying a tray with three mugs on it and a plate of biscuits.

"There's no one about downstairs," he reported, "but I hunted about in the kitchen and found a tin of cocoa, so that's what we've got. How's your head, Tim?"

"A bit sore," said Tim ruefully. "I must say Stewart, you did amazingly well to climb up last night. Those iron rungs at the top were really hard to climb, weren't they?"

Stewart stared.

"Iron rungs? What iron rungs? There weren't any rungs, Tim – just a path, all the way up. It did zigzag about a bit, I'll grant you that, but it was the same path all the way up."

"There *were* rungs, Stewart. It was windy, and cold, and raining, and dark, and...I couldn't see, except when there were flashes of lightning and then only a bit, but...I was climbing iron rungs, up to the flag and—"

Tim stopped. The others stared at him.

"You've been dreaming, Tim," said Stewart. "I expect it was the knock on the head. You probably dreamt all that flag business while you were unconscious and now it seems real to you."

Tim was frowning, trying to remember.

"I didn't dream it. I know I didn't. I was climbing for the flag, at the castle...I...I *wasn't myself*! I think...I was the Prince, getting the flag for Irene. But that makes no sense, no sense at all - why should that suddenly happen? I started out as Tim McTavish, climbing the cliff to rescue Miss Moondancer, and I ended up as Prince Ruhal, reliving his last climb up the castle walls. It just makes no sense at all..."

"You know what I think happened?" Kelly said. "This lantern was burning last night, Tim, in my room. I suppose Mum or Dad put it in here. As you climbed the cliff, you were getting close to the house – to the lantern. We don't know what the lantern's range is. Maybe you don't have to be too close for it to work. Maybe it was having its effect as you climbed."

"Yeah, maybe," said Tim. He didn't sound convinced. "Anyway, what happened to you last night? You were awfully difficult to wake this morning."

Kelly told the others what had happened. It was a long story and she had to stop several times to catch her breath, since her chest still hurt terribly.

Tim and Stewart listened, their faces grave. When she came to the bit about how a second rock fall had opened up an exit from the secret passage, Stewart suddenly banged his fist on the bedside table.

"I told you!" he said. "She's a witch! And when we were on the beach last night, she was uttering spells as well – I heard her. Well, I heard her muttering, anyway. I couldn't make out what she was saying. I bet that's what made you think you were the Prince, Tim. She'd put a spell on you!"

"I think that's absolute nonsense," said Tim. "If she'd wanted to put a spell on me, she could've turned me into a mouse or something whenever she wanted. Anyway, I asked her last night if she was a witch – while we were waiting for you, Stewart. I said that some people in the village thought she was."

"Huh," said Stewart. "She denied it, of course?"

"Yes," said Tim. "At least—"

He stopped, and frowned again.

"Well...what she actually said was, people have always thought she was a witch and if she knew a magic spell to get her home, naturally, she'd use it," he said slowly.

"Aha!" said Stewart. He had a triumphant look in his eye.

"But," said Tim, "she said it in a way that made me think that of course she wasn't a witch, and I still don't think she is. Anyway, carry on, Kelly."

Kelly continued. Stewart did not interrupt again.

"I don't exactly remember what happened right at the end," she said. "I was trying to get in front of the horse, to get it to rear up, and throw Baku off, but I was shot and... that was that. I suppose the soldiers saved them."

Kelly's shoulders shook a little as she relived the experience, but she managed to keep her voice steady, and blinked back the tears. Tim came and sat by her and put his arm around her as she finished.

"Well," he said. "I think that at least proves that Miss Moondancer isn't a witch, or she'd have said a spell and got them out of trouble."

He looked down at his sister.

"You've been through a lot, Kelly. What you did was very brave – braver than I would have been, I think. I'm proud of you, sis."

Kelly smiled at the unexpected praise.

"Also, I think you're right about the lantern," Tim continued. "We can't – mustn't – use it again. It would be much too dangerous. We'd better put it away and forget about it." He sighed. "It's just a pity we never found that key, the key to the jewel box."

At the mention of the jewel box, Kelly began to think – think hard. She *had* seen something, hadn't she. But what?

Then it came to her. She clutched Tim's arm.

"Tim, I saw it! Aunt Irene had the key in a little carved wooden box, I saw her put it in her pocket whilst they were in the castle, packing, and I recognised the box. It's the sandalwood box on the living room mantelpiece down-stairs!"

They all three looked at each other for a second. Then Tim and Stewart jumped up and rushed downstairs, Kelly following more slowly – it hurt her to move too fast. They burst into the living room. The curtains were drawn but Tim switched on the electric light. They crowded to the mantelpiece.

It was empty. There, in the centre, where the box had stood, was just a bare patch.

"It's gone! That break-in we had," Tim said grimly. "When we thought nothing had been stolen, they must've taken the box!"

"Master McTavish," came a voice from the couch, "is this what you're looking for?"

*C*HAPTER *N*INETEEN

They had forgotten about Miss Moondancer – forgotten that she was sleeping on the living room couch. Now they saw that she was holding the carved wooden box.

"Miss Moondancer!" gasped Tim. "Sorry to wake you." His eyes were on the box. "But where did you get that box?"

Miss Moondancer blushed, her face a delicate shade of pink.

For a while, no one spoke. The three children stared at her, a growing suspicion in their minds.

Then Kelly said, "Miss Moondancer, you can't be... you're not...the thief...from the break-in...are you?"

Miss Moondancer's gaze, normally so direct and piercing, for once had lost its lance-like quality. It faltered; she looked down at the floor.

After a second or so she said, "Kelly McTavish, that is a preposterous suggestion." But her tone of voice was such that it sounded for all the world like an admission of guilt.

She looked up again, and fixed her eyes on all three children, one by one. Then she sniffed, and tried to rally her forces.

"Children, listen to me. If I were asked by the police how I obtained this box – *if* I were – I might very well say that I found it on the ground, outside your house, during one of my nightly walks. I would add that the thief probably dropped it whilst making his getaway and, children, *if* the police ask me and I give them this explanation, I have absolutely *no doubt* that they will believe me. After all, I am over seventy years old, a school mistress, and a respected member of the community. About the last person in the village to go around breaking into people's homes."

She sniffed again, but her eyes fell back to the floor. The three children looked at each other; and then Kelly looked straight at her teacher.

"Miss Moondancer, why did you take the key?" she asked.

"She took it to get the treasure, of course," said Stewart triumphantly, before Miss Moondancer could answer. "You stole the key, didn't you, Miss Moondancer, so that you could open the jewel box and take the treasure, without anybody knowing. You thought you'd find the treasure in the house, didn't you? But you couldn't find it, so you kept the key hoping that one day you'd get a chance to search properly. You're a thief, Miss Moondancer – nothing but a common thief!"

Miss Moondancer looked defeated. Her eyes could not meet Stewart's.

"Irene said that if anything were to happen to her, the treasure would be mine," she said in a low voice. "Stewart, Irene was given that treasure by her Prince. It meant everything to her. It was her dowry and every year she'd say to me, 'Agnes, for Ruhal's sake, when I'm gone, please keep this treasure safe and remember our times in India together...'

"She said this to me for the last time a few months ago, as we walked over the hills together. She hadn't been well and I suppose she thought that her time left might be limited. She said she'd written it in her will.

"I don't know why she changed her mind, but after she died and I got a copy of her will from her lawyers, I saw that a few days after my conversation with her, she'd changed her will, and left the treasure to you..."

"I was angry, children. I had no right to be, I see that now, but I was. I was her best friend. You were distant relatives down south who she'd never even met. You had *no idea* of what Irene went through to get the treasure, or what it meant to her. You knew nothing about her and I imagined that you cared even less.

"So, when that key came into my possession, I kept it. But, Tim and Kelly, I was wrong. I've got to know you both over the past few weeks. You might not realise it but you have a lot of Irene about you, Tim, and you too, Kelly. You're not Irene, of course, but you are her family and that means a lot. Last night on the beach, you saved my life,

Tim. So, if there's any treasure to be had," – she smiled faintly – "I want you to have it."

Kelly and Tim went and sat on the floor by the couch where Miss Moondancer was reclining. Kelly said gently, "And you saved Aunt Irene's life, out in India, Miss Moondancer. But for you, she'd never have escaped."

"And as for last night," said Tim, "I was trying to save your life, Miss Moondancer, but I've a suspicion that you saved mine instead."

Miss Moondancer's eyes twinkled at that, but she said nothing.

"I think we should share it," said Kelly firmly, and Tim nodded.

"Well, come on," said Stewart. "What are we waiting for?"

*

The old treasure chest sat on the living-room floor, brought up, with some difficulty, from the cellar by Stewart and Tim. Mum and Dad, awoken by the commotion, sat in armchairs which had been placed each side of the sofa holding Miss Moondancer.

The adults watched quietly. Mum had tried to ask about the box and where the children had found it, but Miss Moondancer had looked straight at her and said, rather surprisingly, "Mrs McTavish, I think children should be allowed their little secrets, don't you? I'm sure that Tim and Kelly will be pleased to tell you all about it in their own time and in their own way, when they see fit."

With that rebuke, Mum shut up, and watched quietly with Dad.

Now, Miss Moondancer pulled the sandalwood box from her pocket again, opened it, and handed the key to Kelly.

The lock turned easily. Kelly lifted the lid, and peered inside. There was a collective holding of breaths. No one spoke.

And then Kelly reached down inside the box and pulled out a handful of diamonds.

*

The floor was covered with treasure. Precious stones, jewellery, ornaments and trinkets of gold and silver surrounded them.

"Aunt Irene's treasure," mumbled Dad. "So it was true, after all."

"Oh, it was true all right, Dad," said Tim. "Aunt Irene wasn't barmy, whatever *you* may have thought."

"She certainly wasn't," agreed Miss Moondancer. "This treasure came from India, Mr McTavish. Your aunt went through a great deal to bring it home."

Dad stared at the treasure.

"This must be worth a fortune," he said.

"Several fortunes," said Tim with a grin. "We're rich, Dad!"

Dad's face broke into a grin. "I think you're right about that," he said. "You know, it might be early, but I've a bottle of champagne stashed away. I think this calls for a celebration, don't you?"

Mrs Rabb entered the room bearing a tray of tea and toast.

"Breakfast time," she said calmly. "You make a start on this, dearies, while I rustle up some bacon and eggs. There's a lot o' you this morning – lucky the larder's full!"

"Mrs Rabb," said Kelly happily. "Look, we're rich!"

Mrs Rabb turned and saw the treasure scattered all over the living-room floor but instead of surprise, admiration, or awe, she simply laughed.

"Och aye, I see that you've found it," she said. "That's Miss Irene's treasure, no doubt about that. 'Tis such a shame it's not the real thing."

"Not the real thing!" cried Kelly. "You're wrong, Mrs Rabb. Of course it's real. I saw—"

She stopped, just in time.

"Och no, dearie," said Mrs Rabb calmly and gently. "That's just what Miss Irene said. She'd thought it genuine all these years, brought it back from India and faced goodness knows how many dangers to get it here. She kept it hidden in the cellar for years. Sometimes – not very often, but sometimes – she used to get it out, bring it up to the kitchen and spread it all over the kitchen table. Then we'd get the gold and silver polish out, and polish it till it shone. Sometimes Miss Irene'd be sad, but mostly we'd talk and laugh about it. 'All this wealth,' she used to say. 'It's too much for an old spinster like me! Eh, Mrs Rabb?'

And we'd look at it one more time and then hide it away in the cellar again.

"Then a few weeks before she died, she got some experts down from Edinburgh to tell her how much it was worth. They took one look and then told her they were paste – all fakes, although very cleverly done.

"I never saw Miss Irene so depressed. She didn't speak for a long time. She just stared into space. Then finally she just said one thing: 'Mrs Rabb, nothing in India is as it seems. Just you remember that, next time *your* Prince gives you a wedding gift.' She was ever so disappointed, she was – ever so. I don't think she got over it, really I don't.

"Now," she said, looking around the room at the sea of silent faces staring at her. "It's breakfast time and such a beautiful day outside. So who's for some nice, crisp, bacon and eggs?"

EPILOGUE

The following day, after breakfast, they walked down the hill to the churchyard, just the two of them, Kelly clutching a posy of freshly picked flowers. The weather had changed again. Low clouds hung in a leaden sky, the air full of moisture. It was one of those days when you couldn't tell when the mist stopped and the rain began. A cool breeze blew in from the sea; the air smelt new, fresh, clean.

They walked silently, each absorbed in their own thoughts, thinking over the events of the past few weeks and days – now and fifty years ago. They walked separately, yet each twin knew what the other felt and thought, their special bond very strong at that moment.

They entered the cemetery through the churchyard gate and began to walk slowly through the graves, seeing and feeling the cool colours around them: grey sky, grey-blue sea, white gulls, green grass. Behind them, the church, slate-grey, and then, facing them, was a stark, white, bright new gravestone.

IRENE
MCTAVISH

BORN 1917
DIED 1986

R.I.P.

"How can you sum up someone's life, just like that?" asked Tim, reading it.

Kelly didn't answer. Instead, she stepped forward and laid her flowers down on the grave. There was another posy already there. She wondered who had laid it – someone from the village, probably.

They stood silently for a moment, the soft highlands mist around them.

"We should have come before," Kelly said quietly. "Do you realise, Tim, this is the closest we've ever been to Aunt Irene?"

Tim reached out and took her hand and then they stood in silence again, thinking of her, this aunt they'd never met in real life, but knew well from their dreams. Thinking of her hopeless love for an Indian Prince and the sadness of her final betrayal, only weeks before.

It must have been really raining, not just misty, for their cheeks were wet as they left the churchyard.

*

As they walked up the road towards home, they heard a shout behind them. Tim turned. It was Conall, the boy from school.

Tim braced for a fight. It had been coming all term, he knew.

Instead, Conall approached them awkwardly. He looked down at the ground.

"I...heard what you did for Miss Moondancer," he said. "Stewart told me. Er... thanks."

Tim nodded. He didn't know what to say.

"Tim, Kelly, it's Guy Fawkes on Saturday," said Conall, "and I'm having a few friends over and some fireworks. D'you two want to come? Say, about six o'clock?"

Tim and Kelly smiled at Conall. His eyes met theirs for the first time.

"See you Saturday then."

*

They trudged up the long hill towards home, not speaking, each immersed in their own thoughts. Kelly's rib still hurt. The doctor attending Miss Moondancer had examined Kelly to see how she was doing with the flu, and when she had complained of the sharp pain in her chest he had prodded her, none too gently, in the side.

Seeing her flinch, he had felt her ribs.

"It's cracked," he said, a little surprised. "You must have broken a rib coughing. It's quite possible to do that, you know."

Kelly knew perfectly well how she'd come to have a broken rib, but she simply nodded and let the doctor prescribe painkillers.

The lantern had been safely put away at the back of a high cupboard in Tim's room. Neither of them wanted to use it again. Even Stewart had agreed.

As they walked home, Tim was still thinking about the treasure. After all that Aunt Irene had been through, it seemed so unfair that the jewels had turned out to be fake. Then something stirred in his mind. He thought back to his time in the jungle encampment, to a conversation he'd overheard.

"Kelly," he said, "it wasn't Prince Ruhal who gave the fakes to Aunt Irene. Well, it was, but he didn't know they were fake."

Kelly turned to him.

"Who was it?"

"It was Queen Shikari," said Tim. "She sent Suhaila, her lady-in-waiting, down to Delhi with the treasure – to have a copy made, no doubt. I heard them plotting it, when I was in the jungle."

"I see – so Ruhal *didn't* mean to deceive Irene," said Kelly.

"No," said Tim. "But – but I suppose, when she found out it was fake she thought that he did, that he was cheating her with the treasure, just like everything else. No wonder she was so sad."

"Yes, and it's clear now why she left the treasure to us. She had her pride, did Aunt Irene. She felt she couldn't tell Miss Moondancer that the treasure was fake, not after all that fuss she made to get it home, so she just changed her will quietly."

"Yes, and we got lucky. Or so we thought."

"She must have known she was dying," said Kelly. "I suppose that's why she got in the experts in the first place. She probably wanted to know how much death duty there'd be."

"Yeah," said Tim, absently.

They had arrived back at the house and to his surprise, a smart black Mercedes was parked outside.

"The lunch guests, remember?" said Kelly. "You know, the people who were supposed to be staying with Miss Moondancer?"

Tim thought. He did remember Miss Moondancer saying something about expecting guests, that time when she'd come for tea. It seemed like years ago now.

"Since Miss Moondancer can't look after her guests, Mum invited them here instead," said Kelly. "They're coming for lunch and then, maybe, to stay."

"Well, who are they?" asked Tim, only mildly interested.

Kelly shrugged her shoulders. "Some boring old grown-ups, I suppose."

Tim pushed open the front door and then stopped in absolute surprise. From the living room came familiar voices – voices that hadn't changed in fifty years.

*

"Tim and Kelly, I'd like you to meet two old friends of mine."

Miss Moondancer, now hobbling on crutches and with her ankle in plaster, was her normal acerbic self.

"Here, children, are their royal highnesses, Princess Ashwina and Princess Pari of the Royal Kingdom of Kimbustan," she said. "Ashwina, Pari, this is Tim and Kelly McTavish; Irene's great nephew and niece."

The two middle-aged, even elderly, ladies, standing in their living room looked almost nothing like the girls they knew. But then Kelly saw Ashwina nudge Pari and both of them giggled in a most familiar way.

"Why, you do look surprised," said Ashwina. "Didn't you know we were coming?"

Tim opened his mouth to reply, but before he could do so Mrs Rabb burst into the room, and to their great surprise she flung her arms around Ashwina and Pari in turn and hugged them until the tears rolled down their cheeks.

"Mrs Rabb!" Mum said in surprise. "What on earth..."

"Och, forgive me, do," said Mrs Rabb, releasing Pari at last. "But it's such a long time since I've seen these wee bairns – such a long time indeed."

"But—"

"Mrs McTavish," said Ashwina. "We've known your Mrs Rabb for years. We used to live here, you see, years ago. In this house. With Aunt Irene."

*

Lunch was over.

Tim and Kelly walked along the cliff tops with Ashwina and Pari. It had stopped raining and the sun was trying to peep through gaps in the clouds. Mrs Rabb was clearing up and preparing "a wee spot of tea", as she called it. Mum and Dad were keeping Miss Moondancer company back in the house.

"After your Great-aunt left the castle," Ashwina was saying, "life was pretty horrible. Our grandmother was very strict. Luckily, Charika kept us out of trouble and kept Grandmother away from us. That wasn't too difficult as it happens. Grandmother's main interest was politics or, putting it bluntly, power. Our small brother Jaideep was Prince Regent, but till he was eighteen it was Grandmother who held the real power and that was what she wanted.

"As it happened, she didn't get what she wanted for very long. She died a few months after our father Ruhal – a heart attack, Charika told us. That was when we got the letter."

"Letter?"

"Yes." Pari took up the story. "We both got a letter from your Great-aunt Irene asking us to come and live with her here in Scotland. So, of course we did. We had nothing to keep us in India. Jaideep had been sent to a boarding school in England by then anyway, arranged by the British government in order to 'learn the ways of the English gentleman', as the British High Commissioner put it. Your Aunt Irene and Agnes Moondancer arranged for us to attend the same boarding school near Edinburgh that they had both gone to. It's only an hour by train from here. So it worked out well. We lived with your aunt here in this house during school holidays – and most weekends too during term time."

"So," Kelly said slowly, "she wasn't alone here? She wasn't unhappy or lonely?"

Ashwina and Pari looked at each other. "Lonely?" said Ashwina, raising an eyebrow, and they both burst into giggles.

"Oh, the times we had here – Irene and Agnes and Mrs Rabb and ourselves – and sometimes Jaideep would come to stay, too, and sometimes Charika, from India. Oh no," Ashwina smiled, "this house was full of laughter, not tears."

"Ashwina, if I may call you that," said Tim, "what happened to the treasure – the real treasure, I mean?"

Over lunch they had told of Irene's will, and the fake treasure they had found.

Ashwina sighed. "You were quite right, Tim, our grandmother did have it copied, secretly," she said. "And it was substituted for the real treasure a few days before Ruhal presented it to your aunt. He never knew it was fake of course. The Queen had done it to preserve the wealth of the crown from the British, and she certainly did not tell her son.

"Once Irene and Agnes had gone, the Queen arranged for the real treasure to be put back in its normal place in the castle strong-room. Not many people realised that Ruhal had attempted to give it to Irene – and those who did know were told simply that the treasure had been recovered, left behind by the cowardly fleeing British girls."

"So it's still there - it belongs to you now?"

"Oh, no," said Pari. "Not any more. You see, the British left in 1947 when India and Kimbustan declared independence. That was the end of British rule – but the end of the monarchy as well. Kings and queens were no longer to rule over the people of Kimbustan. An elected government came to power, and the first thing they did was to seize the treasure which they said belonged to all the people of Kimbustan, not just the royal family. Most of it was sold and what gold was left was melted down. We lost our castle too and our palace, seized by the government – it's now a very luxurious hotel, would you believe?"

"Luckily, our grandmother hadn't put quite all the genuine treasure back in the strong room," said Ashwina, with a twinkle in her eye. "A few pieces were...kept back."

"Um," said Tim, thinking of the black Mercedes – the latest model – parked outside the house. "I see."

"You know, Ashwina and I were talking on the flight over here," said Pari. "India is not what it was – not at all – and since we've lived a lot of our lives already in these parts, we rather thought we might look for a house around here – settle down in Scotland, you might say."

Tim grinned at Kelly and she smiled back. Ashwina giggled.

"You two look like a couple of Cheshire cats with grins like that," she said. "Oh, I think we'll have fun, children, don't you?"

Kelly grinned again, at Ashwina this time.

"You know, I hated it when we first moved here," she said. "But now I think I'm going to like it – like it a great deal, I think."

"Yes," said Tim, nodding. "Even school won't be so bad. Even Miss Moondancer—"

He stopped, frowned and then turned to Ashwina and Pari.

"Well, I suppose you should know, as well as anybody," he said. "Is – is our teacher a witch?"

There was a sudden pause. He saw Pari look at Ashwina.

"In India, we see things differently to you," Ashwina said, at length. "Here, if anything is strange, or you can't explain it, you think it's magic and therefore to be feared. In Kimbustan, magic is all around us. We do not fear it. We do not try to explain it. It is the norm, not the exception. And therefore if we believe that someone has a power to change things, a power that we cannot explain, we simply shrug our shoulders and hope they use their power wisely.

"Whether your teacher is or is not a witch does not matter. What matters is what they do with such a power, not whether they possess it or not."

The sun had gone behind a cloud now and it was suddenly cold. Tim shivered, and then he felt something deep, deep down come awake, and stir again in his soul, as it had that summer's day, long ago, back in England.

He glanced at Ashwina and Pari, dressed in their perfectly simple, well cut, stylish black dresses and realised, as he did so, that their hawk's eyes, their keen, sharp, piercing, twinkling eyes were pools of pure black – jet black, witches' black, just like their grandmother's, just like Miss Moondancer's.

"And that reminds me," Pari added, "Ashwina, we should tell them the reason for our visit."

Ashwina reached into her pocket, produced a small packet and held it out to Kelly.

"Irene wrote to me, a few weeks before she died," she said. "She asked me to bring you – this."

Inside was a small carved pendant, on a simple gold chain.

"It is the amulet; my father's amulet," said Ashwina. "Kelly, Miss Moondancer has told us that you are...suitable, very suitable. She thinks, also, that you are ready, and that you may be trusted. So, take the amulet: wear it wisely, my child, and guard it with your life."

The two ladies dressed all in black, surrounded Kelly now, and Tim, watching from outside the circle, felt once more an indefinable sense of dread, or fear rise within him as the sun glinted off the thing in Kelly's hand.

Kelly held up the pendant and saw that the carving was

of a tiger, with something – a flag? – in its mouth. And as she looked at it and lifted it to fasten around her neck, she saw the tiger slowly turn its head, look at her and wink.

But she must have been mistaken, mustn't she? It was only a stone carving, after all...

This novel began life as a light-hearted short story. Somehow, it grew, and in the process it became a much deeper and darker work. For the curious, there is no coded message, secret meaning or hidden agenda – this tale is simply to be taken at face value. It may not make complete sense – but real life frequently doesn't.

The antecedents to this story are as follows:

In the summer of 1992, our own youthful adventures behind us, my wife and I bought a big old house, high in the hills of Pinner, overlooking not the sea, but the golf course.

In a dusty corner of the attic, long abandoned, lay an old chest. My children dubbed this "the treasure chest" but it contained no treasure, at least none of the conventional kind. It did house several old dresses and frocks from the 1920's and 1930's; and tucked into a corner, an old invitation from the "King-emporer (sic) and Queen Empress" of India, to a New Years' Eve ball, in Calcutta, in 1912. "Full court dress to be worn." The chest now has pride of place in our living room. It did not contain a rusty old oil lamp, but an acquaintance from the Middle East had presented me with that genuine article several years previously. Then, as now, it adorns our downstairs cloakroom.

All the characters in this story, the locations and, of course, the plot itself are entirely fictitious, save for two incidents.

One hot summer night, for fun, I invited my two daughters to sleep in a tent in the back garden with me. Shortly after midnight, the mother and father of all thunderstorms broke. My daughters awoke terrified. In torrential rain, I carried my youngest daughter through the storm to the house. She has been frightened of thunderstorms ever since.

Some years before, we had taken a short holiday by the seaside. Walking along a cliff top path one sunny morning with my son, then four or five years old, we spotted a steep and precipitous path down to the beach below. We both attempted the descent; he slipped and fell some thirty feet or so. He landed harmlessly in some bracken, but the memory of his fall has stayed with him, and me, over the intervening years.